About the Author

It was as a teacher and parent that Rose Impey first started telling her own stories, and they were so well received she soon started writing them down. Rose writes fantastic books for all ages – she wrote the bestselling *Sleepover Club* books for younger readers and *Hothouse Flower*, *My Scary Fairy Godmother* and *The Shooting Star* are three of her wonderful books for older readers.

Rose lives in Leicestershire.

Other books by Rose Impey:

Hothouse Flower
My Scary Fairy Godmother
The Shooting Star

To Millie, Karen and Kaia – three great drama queens

Sincere thanks also to Alice Duncan, Peter Huff-Rouselle,
Diana Wilkes, Roger Harris, Nadine Hossent and all the
wonderful students from the many drama groups I visited.

ORCHARD BOOKS
338 Euston Road, London NW1 3BH
Orchard Books Australia
Hachette Children's Books
Level 17/207 Kent Street, Sydney, NSW 2000

ISBN 978 1 84616 706 5

A paperback original
First published in 2008

Text © Rose Impey 2008

The right of Rose Impey to be identified as
the author of this work has been asserted by her in
accordance with the Copyright, Designs and Patents Act, 1988.

A CIP catalogue record for this book is available from the British Library.

1 3 5 7 9 10 8 6 4 2

Printed in Great Britain

Orchard Books is a division of Hachette Children's Books,
an Hachette Livre UK company

www.orchardbooks.co.uk

INTRODUCING

ROSE IMPEY

ORCHARD BOOKS

Chapter One

All the world's a stage...

For Scarlett Lee, the whole wide world was a stage. And, to the dismay of her long-suffering family, Scarlett's favourite stage of all was the kitchen at home.

She burst in now, fresh from Drama Club, threw her bag to the floor and announced triumphantly, 'Can you believe it? We're doing *Othello!*'

Crossing the kitchen, Scarlett pulled open a drawer and grabbed the first thing that came to hand – a plastic spatula. She stabbed herself viciously with it, fortunately into her armpit.

'No way but this...' she declared, falling heavily to the floor, 'killing myself, to die upon a kiss!' Scarlett groaned convincingly, then lay there perfectly still – almost, but not quite, dead.

'I do wish you wouldn't roll on the floor in

that new T-shirt,' sighed her mum, Jenny, busy preparing supper.

Scarlett ignored the unwanted interruption and gave a few more heart-rending groans. She concluded her performance with not one, but two long last gasps: 'Ahhh! Ahhhhh!' – before finally expiring.

Scarlett had pretty well perfected the art of dying. She practised daily, dropping to the floor as if she hadn't a bone in her body.

'Watch me! Watch me die!' she routinely begged anyone who came to the house. Scarlett had a variety of methods, but stabbing was currently her favourite.

'Wonderful,' said her mum, giving a short burst of applause. 'Now perhaps you'll get up.' She retrieved the less-than-lethal spatula and returned it to the drawer.

'Oh, not that old Dying Swan routine again,' complained Cleo, Scarlett's fifteen-year-old sister, coming into the kitchen. Obliged to step over Scarlett to reach the fridge, Cleo took the opportunity to tread briefly on her sister's ponytail.

Scarlett cried out in pain, for real this time, 'Mu-u-um! Tell her!'

'Please, girls!' their mother sighed. 'Keep the noise down.'

'*Drama Queen*,' Cleo mouthed at Scarlett.

'*Thanks*,' Scarlett mouthed back, taking this as a compliment.

Scarlett was happy to admit it: she *was* a full-on, five-star, blockbuster of a drama queen. Wasn't she named after Scarlett O'Hara – one of the greatest drama queens ever? With her mum she had watched *Gone with the Wind* a dozen times and knew whole chunks of it by heart.

Their favourite bit was the ending, where Rhett Butler finally leaves and Scarlett asks in a pathetic voice, 'But what about me, Rhett? What will I do?' and Rhett walks out saying, 'Frankly, my dear, I don't give a da-a-amn.'

At school, Scarlett was famous for being a colossal show-off, which caused her sister a good deal of embarrassment.

'Don't you even *care* what people think?' Cleo often asked in desperation.

But Scarlett merely raised one eyebrow – a habit that drove her sister crazy – stroked an imaginary moustache, and said in her best Rhett Butler voice,

'Frankly, my dear, I don't give a da-a-amn.'

And Scarlett really, really didn't.

According to her parents, even as a baby she had always loved an audience. As soon as she could walk, she had learned to take a bow, and by the age of two was already singing into a hairbrush in front of a mirror.

At the age of five Scarlett had grabbed the microphone at a family wedding and entertained one hundred guests with a performance of 'My Heart Will Go On' from *Titanic*, her hair thrown back in the face of the wind. As her mum often remarked: Celine Dion had a lot to answer for.

Now – at the great age of thirteen – there was no doubt left in anyone's mind, least of all Scarlett's, that *it was her destiny* to become A VERY GREAT ACTRESS!

And what was the one thing that every great actress needed? A loyal audience, of course. Enter stage right: Scarlett's best friend, Gemma.

Gemma and Scarlett had become friends when they both joined Drama Club two years earlier. Right from the start it had been evident that, unlike Scarlett, Gemma was not a natural actress. In their first production Scarlett had been chosen to play

Julius Caesar, the leading role, while Gemma had been merely a spear-carrier. Two years later, on-stage and off, Gemma was still playing the spear-carrier to Scarlett's emperor: never failing to laugh at Scarlett's jokes, gasp at her often outrageous behaviour and loudly applaud her impressions of their teachers and friends at school.

Gemma was, undoubtedly, the ideal best friend for Scarlett – as well as her loyal follower.

Only a few hours earlier the two girls had arrived at Drama Club as they usually did: Scarlett leading the way, demanding everyone's attention as she made her entrance, acknowledging her imagined fans on all sides – *thank you, thank you* – and Gemma bringing up the rear, trying not to feel too embarrassed by her friend's eccentric behaviour.

The other girls rolled their eyes, as they often did around Scarlett, but couldn't resist smiling, before returning to their conversations while they awaited Mr Coe's arrival.

Drama Club met on Tuesdays and Thursdays after school in an old, rather run-down outbuilding. Tucked away from the main school, it gave the girls a warm, private place to while away break times, free from the interference of teachers. This was one of the perks of being a member of Mr Coe's Drama Club and for some of the girls the main reason they had joined.

This was not true of Scarlett, of course, who was deadly serious about acting. While the others gossiped and giggled she settled down to follow Mr Coe's advice: that to be good actors, they must first become good observers.

'Watch and learn, girls,' he had told them. 'Watch and learn.'

Scarlett had taken these words quite literally and turned overnight into a serious people-watcher – even in cafes, to her sister's further embarrassment!

'For goodness' sake, stop showing us up,' Cleo would hiss across the table, as Scarlett perfectly copied the lady on the next table as she nibbled her way daintily around a large doughnut, looking exactly like a squirrel.

Now, Scarlett applied the same close scrutiny to her friends in Drama Club. First checking that none of them was watching, she nudged Gemma.

'Who's this?' she whispered.

Scarlett sat up straight and pushed out her chest,

tilting her head to one side. She licked her lips and pressed them lightly together in a pout, widening her eyes until she looked like Bambi.

Gemma, stifling a giggle, whispered back, 'Zara!'

Zara sat a few metres away, blissfully unaware. She was probably the easiest of the girls to mimic. With blonde hair, tanned skin and a perfect figure, Zara was by far the most glamorous girl in their year – and the most vain. Although they weren't allowed to wear make-up at school, Zara always carried a pot of lip-gloss, which she constantly reapplied. She had even been known to tuck it down the front of her swimsuit for use in the swimming pool.

Scarlett closed her eyes and moved seamlessly into a second improvisation, where she silently played a set of drums, swaying from side to side in time to the music that seemed to be playing inside her head.

Gemma grinned and flicked her eyes in Leah's direction. When Leah looked their way, Scarlett hastily stopped drumming and gave her a smile and a friendly wave.

For her next impersonation Scarlett was happy to have everyone's attention. Their drama teacher was a small, anxious-looking man who was already losing his hair. Scarlett jumped up and paced about the room, perfectly mimicking the way he raked his fingers through what little hair he had left until it stood up vertically on his head like a Mohican. 'Girls, girls!' she bellowed at them. 'Give it some *fizz*!'

Scarlett felt gratified by the ripple of laughter – and applause – that followed. She was taking a few bows when they heard the teacher's hurried footsteps coming down the corridor. Everyone stifled their laughter and Scarlett hastily rearranged her face.

Despite sometimes mimicking Mr Coe, Scarlett was actually his biggest fan. When she first met him she thought she had died and gone to actors' heaven. Scarlett's previous experience – at a Saturday morning Drama Club – had been deeply disappointing. She had spent half of the first session pretending to be the sausage in a fried breakfast and the other half as the fork. She'd come home utterly disgusted and told her parents, 'Don't ever send me back to that dodgy place. That teacher was crazy!'

So Scarlett had been just aching to meet someone like Mr Coe, someone who would take her ambitions seriously. Mr Coe was certainly serious, if not passionate, about drama himself. He had very firm views on acting and believed in throwing his students in at the deep end.

'I know some people might consider Shakespeare too difficult for twelve- and thirteen-year-olds,' he had told them, 'but I have no patience with that view.'

Mr Coe thought that Shakespeare was little short of God and Scarlett soon agreed with him.

So she was utterly thrilled at the end of the session, when Mr Coe announced that their next production would be scenes from *Othello*. Some of the other girls were less enthusiastic and one or two quietly groaned, but Scarlett could hardly wait to give her family the exciting news, especially her dad.

Although Scarlett's dad, Steve, often worked away from home, sometimes for weeks at a time, he tried to call most evenings. When he rang that night, after supper, it was the first thing Scarlett told him.

'*Othello*?! That's a bit heavy isn't it?' he said.

Steve wasn't exactly a keen theatregoer. Sitting through anything for more than an hour, unless it was a rugby match, caused his eyes to close. He was often in trouble with the rest of the family for snoring and showing them up in public.

'We're not doing the *whole* play,' Scarlett explained,

'just a few scenes. Mr Coe's adapted it. He's calling it: *Scenes of a Betrayal.*' She gave the title plenty of dramatic emphasis.

'I suppose there'll be lots of dying in it?' said her dad.

Scarlett was used to being teased about her fondness for a gruesome death scene. 'Yeah!' she said enthusiastically. 'Most of the cast are dead on the bed at the end. It'll be rocking. Anyway, it's not for a few weeks yet, ' she added. 'You'll be home by then, won't you?'

Scarlett heard the slightest hesitation before he said, 'Well...maybe. It all depends...'

Before Scarlett could ask what it depended upon, her mum signalled that her time was up.

Scarlett quickly said, 'Gotta go, Dad. Smile! Be Happy! Love you lots,' and turned off her phone.

Scarlett's dad was a financial advisor. He had his own business, with an office in town and another in Malaga, in Spain, where he advised British people who'd moved out there how to invest their money.

Whenever the girls complained about him being away from home so much, Steve reminded them that by helping his rich clients to become even richer, he hoped to become rich too. As soon as that happened he planned to take a year off and they would all sail around the world together. This had been her dad's dream for as long as Scarlett could remember. But even this possibility didn't stop Scarlett from wishing him home!

While their mum talked to their dad, Scarlett and Cleo sat at opposite ends of the sofa pulling faces at one another.

'So what part are you after?' Cleo asked sarcastically. 'Othello, I suppose.'

'Why not?' Scarlett asked. The fact that she went to an all girls' school meant that she was never in competition with boys for the male leads.

'Why not!' Cleo laughed. 'Because Othello is *black* is why not.'

'So?' Scarlett replied.

'So, dream on,' Cleo said, giving her sister a superior look which Scarlett perfectly mirrored back.

'You'll go too far one of these days,' Cleo warned her, 'and then you'll be sorry.'

Their mum gave the girls a warning look and they both backed off.

Scarlett didn't care in the least that her sister,

like lots of people at school, thought she was a bighead. But she knew Cleo had a point about Othello. She retreated to her bedroom to ponder the problem in private and to seek comfort from her journal.

Under Mr Coe's influence Scarlett had been keeping a journal for the last two years. It wasn't meant to be a diary exactly, more a collection of her own thoughts and feelings about acting, a record of her many triumphs and occasional disasters – Scarlett knew that every good actress could learn from those.

She also included any pearls of wisdom that dropped from Mr Coe's lips, or Miss Kitty's, her singing teacher. One day Scarlett fully intended to pass these on to other keen drama students, when she herself was a world-famous star of stage and screen.

Scarlett had noticed that whenever Mr Coe spoke about acting it was as if he were speaking *IN CAPITAL LETTERS*, and this had an unconscious effect on Scarlett's journal entries.

Acting is MY LIFE. It's WHO I AM!

Acting is like having a REALLY, REALLY

interesting conversation where someone's
already told you what to say.

Mr Coe says that every actor has A STORY
and the richer the story the better. I don't
think I have A STORY yet because my life so
far has been pretty boring, but one day
I will have A STORY – and it can't come
soon enough.

Mr Coe had also told the girls that an actor must be *RUTHLESSLY HONEST*. This was something that Scarlett prided herself on. She scrutinised herself in just the same way as she studied other people.

Scarlett was ready to admit that at times she did tend to blather on a bit, and when she got passionate about things she knew that other people thought she was plain *weird*. But she had many positive qualities too and she didn't believe in pretending otherwise. If you were good at something why hide it? That was her attitude.

On the other hand, Scarlett wasn't completely thick-skinned. She hadn't yet admitted to any of the other girls that she'd set her heart on the main role of

Othello – because it wasn't a foregone conclusion that she would get it.

If Cleo was right, the only black girl in the group, Leah, would probably get the part. But Scarlett was relying on the fact that Mr Coe wasn't predictable in that way. He might still give it to the best actress in the group – which everyone knew was her.

When she had confided in Gemma how badly she wanted the part, her best friend had been supremely confident on Scarlett's behalf and reminded her that there was no real competition.

'You're bound to get it. It's a done deal. You're the best; everyone knows that.'

Oh, it was like music to Scarlett's ears. Thank goodness for Gemma, who was bright and intelligent and Scarlett's biggest fan.

But sometimes Scarlett couldn't help wishing that Gemma had a little bit more...*backbone*. When Zara was throwing her weight about, or Brogan was looking for an argument, Gemma rarely stood up for herself. Even with Scarlett, Gemma usually just went along with things.

Strangely, Gemma was the only member of Drama Club that Scarlett didn't mimic, even when

Gemma begged her to do so.

'Why won't you ever do me?'

The truth was her friend didn't really have any obvious mannerisms – nothing Scarlett could hook onto. She was just...Gemma, and deep down, even if she never got round to telling her, Scarlett really did love and appreciate her.

Scarlett knew full well how lucky she was to have a best friend like Gemma – backbone or not!

Chapter Two

Though this be madness, yet there is method in't.

The next time Drama Club met, with the auditions only a week away, there was a sense of excitement and mild hysteria among the girls, which Mr Coe was doing his best to control.

He began that day, as he often did, with a short session of relaxation, which was why they were all lying flat on the floor looking like stranded starfish, with their eyes closed – some of them trying valiantly not to giggle.

'*Breathe…slowly,*' he told them. 'And, for goodness' sake, try to settle down.'

Scarlett ignored the fidgeting going on around her, closed her eyes and faithfully followed Mr Coe's directions.

If Shakespeare was little short of God – in Mr Coe's

view – in Scarlett's eyes Mr Coe came a pretty close second. Most of her opinions on acting began, 'I agree with Mr Coe…'

Scarlett certainly agreed with her teacher that the best way to approach acting was from the inside outwards. This approach was called *The Method*, Mr Coe had explained, and it was first devised by the great Russian director, Stanislavski. It involved an actor using his own feelings and experiences to understand the character he is playing – in some cases going to extraordinary lengths to identify with the part.

'For example, when Robert de Niro played an ageing boxer in the film *Raging Bull*,' Mr Coe had told them, 'he not only learned to box, he wore a false nose and put on sixty pounds.'

'I'm sorry, Mr Coe,' Zara had said, speaking for many of the girls, 'there are some sacrifices I'm prepared to make for acting – but putting on weight isn't one of them!'

Scarlett had rolled her eyes. She continually despaired of girls like Zara, who put vanity before their art. If Mr Coe had directed Scarlett to cut off all her hair she'd have done it like a shot – if it were in the name of drama.

Mr Coe walked around the room, adopting the hushed tones he always used for these relaxation sessions. 'Remember, girls, acting requires a *clear, open* mind at all times. *Open* to new ideas and new experiences.'

The teacher had devised his own version of The Method, which he liked to call The *COE* System: *C for Clear – O for Open – and E for Energised*.

Once he had successfully calmed everyone down, Mr Coe liked to increase the pace, organising them into a couple of fast and furious *energising* games, like Cat and Mouse. The girls found this rather confusing. But, as he often reminded them, *energy* is an actor's secret source of power. It needs to be controlled, he warned, kept under pressure like the bubbles in a bottle of pop. This was probably the reason why one of his favourite directions to the girls was, *'Give it some fizz!'*

Scarlett was getting impatient for the real work to begin. Improvisation was always her favourite part of the lesson and she rolled up her sleeves in readiness.

Mr Coe began today's session with a short explanation of the concept of cloning. He gave the girls five minutes to brainstorm a short scene where

A is walking down a street, only to come face-to-face with B – a perfect clone of herself. How would they each react?

Scarlett, who usually hit the ground running, was slow to get started. She was so gripped with the idea of there being an identical version of Scarlett Lee somewhere else on the planet that she couldn't stop talking about it.

'I mean...it would be like one of those déjà vu moments,' she said, but added, doubtfully, 'although I can't believe she'd be *exactly* like me.'

'Duh! That's the general idea,' Gemma pointed out.

'Wouldn't it just blow your mind?' Scarlett asked no one in particular.

'Not really,' said Gemma, who couldn't see anything especially interesting about meeting up with one's self.

'No offence but...aren't you curious whether you'd even like her? Whether she'd be like your *bestest* ever friend, or if you'd absolutely hate each other on sight?'

Gemma sighed; she just wanted to get on with it.

'It'd be creepy,' Scarlett decided. 'I might feel like murdering her.'

Gemma quietly suggested, 'Mmm, she might have the same idea.'

Suddenly Mr Coe called out, 'OK. Let's get to work, girls.'

'You be the clone,' Scarlett told Gemma, finally getting down to business.

Unusually, Gemma asked why. 'Why can't I be the original?'

Scarlett didn't have any particular reason. 'You just didn't seem bothered about meeting *your* clone,' she shrugged, 'so I thought...'

'Whatever...' Gemma cut her off and walked to the other side of the room.

Scarlett blinked. This wasn't the first time Gemma had seemed a little touchy lately. She sighed and walked in the opposite direction. The girls turned to face one another like two people preparing for a duel. They took several steps forward, before Scarlett suddenly called out, 'Wait! I'm not ready! I haven't worked out my back story.'

Sometimes Mr Coe encouraged the girls to ask themselves who they were in certain situations. Where did they come from? What were they doing there? But today he told Scarlett, 'It's just an exercise!

You don't need a back story. Get on with it, please.'

Scarlett felt frustrated, but quickly came up with one anyway. She would be a single parent who'd just discovered she had a terminal illness and there was no one to look after her children. She walked towards Gemma, clearly weighed down under a blanket of misery, despair and tragedy...

So she wasn't at all prepared for Gemma to demand, rather aggressively in Scarlett's opinion, 'Wha'dya think you're looking at?'

Gemma didn't give Scarlett time to recover before pressing on, 'You can't come down here pretending to be me.'

'I'm not pretending to be *you*!' Scarlett whispered, reminding Gemma what they'd agreed. 'It's the other way round.'

But Gemma ignored her, 'I don't know who you think you are, but *I'm* Scarlett Lee.'

'No, you're not,' Scarlett said, taken aback. 'I am!'

'Prove it!' Gemma demanded, with a flick of her wrist, as if she were throwing down a gauntlet.

Scarlett thought Gemma looked like a character from some TV soap – ready for a fight. She had a strong desire to giggle, not something she normally did in drama sessions, but then Gemma didn't normally take things quite so seriously.

She stifled the giggle because she could see Mr Coe nearby, watching them intently. 'Come on, Scarlett, Gemma's giving you lots to work with here,' he told her. 'Try to keep up.'

Scarlett did try, but having started slowly she never quite recovered. Gemma seemed to be running away with the scene, leaving her best friend limping behind. It was a new and uncomfortable experience for Scarlett.

'Excellent work,' Mr Coe told Gemma at the end of the session. 'I've been wondering when you were going to come out from Scarlett's shadow.'

After the lesson, the girls walked back to Scarlett's house together, Gemma pushing her bike, so that they could work on their audition piece for the following week. Scarlett noticed that Gemma couldn't stop grinning.

'You look like the clone that got the cream,' she told her, not unkindly.

'I know! It was great!' Gemma beamed. 'I really, really enjoyed that.'

'Yeah, you were good,' Scarlett conceded. 'Really good.' But Scarlett couldn't help thinking that if only Mr Coe hadn't rushed her she would have done something equally excellent herself. It was especially hard that it should have happened today when Mr Coe must already be thinking about casting for the next production.

As if she had read Scarlett's mind, Gemma said, 'Don't worry, you're bound to get Othello.'

Scarlett, who was feeling a little less confident than usual, said, 'I hope so.'

'I wonder who'll get to play his wife?' Gemma casually remarked.

Scarlett shrugged, 'Probably Zara. She looks like a Desdemona.'

'Mmm,' Gemma agreed. She left a little silence before adding, almost to herself. 'That's the part I'd like.'

Scarlett was surprised. Gemma had rarely had a speaking role, let alone one of the main characters. She didn't want her friend to get her hopes up, only to be disappointed. 'What about Bianca?' she suggested. It was a much smaller part but she'd still have a few lines.

Gemma turned to Scarlett, looking crushed. 'You don't think I could do it, do you?'

'Yeah...I...I do,' Scarlett said, not quickly enough to be convincing.

'Perhaps if I had extra lessons like you...' Gemma trailed off.

'Well, why don't you?' Scarlett replied.

Gemma ignored this. 'Anyway,' she said, 'Mr Coe said I was *excellent* just now.'

Scarlett thought that might be slightly stretching the truth, but she hastened to reassure her friend. 'And you were. I was just thinking...you might prefer not to have so many lines to learn...you know how nervous you get.'

It was true that Gemma got terrible stage fright. Scarlett, on the other hand, was rarely troubled by nerves and had more than enough self-confidence for the pair of them. *Enough to sink a large battleship,* Cleo often told her – sometimes adding: *probably the whole fleet.*

The girls' audition practice didn't go well. This was partly because every time Scarlett hesitated over her lines, Gemma kept prompting her – just as she was on the point of remembering them.

'Can you give me a *minute*,' Scarlett snapped several times.

'You'll have to learn them before next week,' Gemma reminded her.

'Yes, I think I know that,' Scarlett replied, through gritted teeth. Sometimes Gemma did have a knack for stating the obvious.

In the end Gemma had gone into a bit of a mood and Scarlett had tried to lighten the atmosphere with a couple of her impressions of the other girls.

She did Brogan first. She was much smaller than the other girls and hadn't grown a centimetre since primary school. To compensate she often huffed and puffed like a steam engine before exploding indignantly about some small injustice or other.

'It ain't fair, Mr C,' Scarlett huffed and puffed like Brogan, 'it just ain't fair! Why can't I do the lighting?'

Despite her mood Gemma's face creased into a smile. Encouraged, Scarlett did one of her own favourites: Abbie.

Abbie had once played Mollie, the vain and silly horse from *Animal Farm*, and it seemed to Scarlett that since then she had taken on some of the mannerisms of a young horse herself. Copying her, Scarlett shook her head from side to side, softly neighing, 'My name's *A-bb-ie*.'

Scarlett finally showed Gemma the new one she'd added to her repertoire. 'OK, who's this?' she asked, walking around her bedroom with her bottom sticking out, as if she were balancing a small tray on it.

Gemma grinned, immediately recognising Eve, the new girl at school. She shook her head, impressed. Scarlett had every one of the girls off exactly, although Gemma suspected they wouldn't be very pleased if they knew that. By the time Gemma left Scarlett felt that the atmosphere had been restored.

But moments later Cleo put her head round Scarlett's bedroom door wanting to know what they'd been arguing about.

'We were *not* arguing,' Scarlett insisted. 'Gemma doesn't argue.'

'Even worms can turn,' Cleo replied, cryptically.

Scarlett dismissed Cleo's remark. She reminded herself that her sister knew far more about saving the planet than she did about human psychology. Cleo might be clever and work hard at school, and her devotion to recycling had become almost a religion, but she didn't have Scarlett's ability to understand other people's feelings. In their family, Scarlett was the *people person* – as every Great Actress needed to be.

Later, when Scarlett went down for supper, her mood was immediately improved by finding Uncle Gerry sitting at the table.

'How's my favourite budding Oscar winner?' he asked.

Scarlett had to remind Gerry yet again that real actresses didn't trouble their heads with such matters. She was more interested in becoming a great and serious actress, like...Dame Judi Dench.

'Judi Dench has made stacks of films. And won an Oscar,' Cleo was quick to point out.

'I know *that*,' Scarlett replied. 'Why does *everyone* have to state the obvious?'

'Perhaps in the hope that something might sink in,' Cleo countered. 'Like, for example, just once you might remember that a DVD player uses eighty-five per cent of its electricity when it's not even turned on!'

Scarlett shrugged, as if this were nothing to her. 'So?' she asked.

'So – TURN IT OFF WHEN YOU'VE FINISHED

WATCHING IT!' Cleo bellowed right in her sister's ear.

'Oh, shut up,' Scarlett snapped back.

'Don't tell me to shut up,' Cleo replied.

'Cleo, please don't provoke her,' their mum begged.

'*Me*?! Provoke *her*!' Cleo jumped to her feet and waved her arms around in frustration. 'I don't understand why no one else takes this stuff seriously!'

It looked set to turn into one of the girls' major stand-offs but Gerry – good old Uncle Gerry – leapt to his feet.

'We're on your side,' he told Cleo, 'aren't we, Jenny?' He pulled their mum away from the cooker, turning off every switch in the kitchen including the oven, even though the supper was still cooking.

'Ways to save fuel,' he announced. 'One: don't eat supper, and two: don't eat supper in the dark.' He darted into the hall and returned with armfuls of coats, throwing them at everyone. 'Three: save heating by wearing a coat while not eating supper.'

Scarlett immediately joined in the game, wrapping herself in three layers until she was pink in the face and almost expiring.

'Four: huddle together to conserve body heat,' he said, grabbing them all in a big hug. Cleo pulled away; *she* was determined not to be amused.

But everyone else was amused. They all looked so ridiculous. Scarlett was wearing her own, her mum's and her dad's coats in layers trailing down to the floor; her mum looked like a little Michelin man in Scarlett's ski jacket that barely fastened across her; and Gerry, the most ridiculous of all, was squeezed into Cleo's school blazer with the tea cosy on his head, wearing her mum's yellow rubber gloves.

'Conservation is *not* a laughing matter,' Cleo said, quietly, leaving the kitchen in as dignified a manner as she could, despite tripping over her dad's cagoule on the way out.

Jenny sighed with relief. 'Well done,' she said to Gerry, turning the oven back on. 'Danger averted.'

Uncle Gerry could always be relied on to take the heat out of a situation by turning it into a joke. This was what Scarlett loved about him. And so had Cleo – until, in Scarlett's opinion, she had become an eco-freak and lost her sense of humour.

Gerry wasn't their real uncle. He was their dad's best and oldest friend. He worked in the family business, as a financial director or something or other Scarlett didn't fully understand. When her dad was in Spain,

Gerry kept his eye on things and would often drop in on his way home from work, to check they were all OK.

Gerry had two girls of his own, Olivia and Mariella, and the four girls had been like cousins when they were little. But they saw each other rarely now. Gerry's girls had gone to boarding school after their mum, Patti, had developed MS and was in a wheelchair.

Scarlett sometimes found it hard to believe that Gerry and her dad had been at school together. It wasn't that her dad seemed *old*, exactly, it was more that Gerry seemed so much younger. Scarlett's mum called him Peter Pan. 'I don't think he'll ever grow up,' she would often say.

Another reason why Scarlett loved Gerry was that he *always* showed interest in her acting career. When she told him that they were doing *Othello* he said with relish, 'I remember reading that at school. Lots of juicy death scenes. So what's your part?'

'I'd like Othello,' she said a little coyly, then sighed, 'I'm hoping Dad'll be home in time to see it.'

'Well, that's not looking likely now, is it?' Gerry said.

Scarlett caught a look between Gerry and her mum, followed by the slightest shake of Mum's head. She knew what that gesture meant – don't tell Scarlett *something*. But before she could ask what, Gerry went on, 'I meant, do we know when he's due home?'

'We'll probably have more idea when he rings at the weekend,' Mum said. 'Come on, Scarlett, set the table. Are you going to stay to eat?' she asked Gerry.

Gerry accepted. He was in no rush to get home to an empty house. His wife had gone to a health spa for a few days.

'What bliss,' said Mum a little enviously. The idea of a few days rest and relaxation without two squabbling girls around seemed like her idea of heaven. But, of course, she wouldn't have wanted to be ill, like Patti.

Later that evening, back in her bedroom, Scarlett was annoyed that she hadn't tried to get to the bottom of what that shared look between her mum and Gerry had meant. But it had slipped from her mind because Gerry had kept them entertained all evening. Even Cleo's ice queen act had thawed by the time he left.

Despite all his jokes, Scarlett sometimes felt slightly sorry for Uncle Gerry. She thought he was like one of those clowns who makes everyone else laugh, but underneath the make-up is rather sad. Maybe that was another reason why she and Gerry got on so well, she thought; they were both good actors.

Sitting up in bed, Scarlett considered the possibility that she, too, might be a different person underneath the mask – a deeper, more serious character.

Maybe I am not really this outgoing, self-confident, good fun person, but a tragic, heroic figure – like Othello! Must try to discover WHO IS THE REAL SCARLETT LEE?

Before turning out her light Scarlett finished her journal entry with another of her collection of quotes from The Mighty Bard, this time from *Hamlet*:

To die, to sleep, perchance to dream...

Lights fade... Blackout... Curtains...

Scarlett could never resist a dramatic exit.

Chapter Three

It is the green-eyed monster...

Mr Coe may have been the strongest influence on Scarlett's budding acting career, but he was not the only one. There was also her Voice and Singing teacher, Mrs Jacobs, or as she encouraged her pupils to call her – Miss Kitty.

Miss Kitty was an older lady who had been teaching for a very long time. She had been in and around the theatre for much of her life and had been married to a moderately successful Shakespearean actor called Bernard, whom Kitty described as a *Proper Ac-tor*. She meant as distinct from the type with no posture and no technique that mumbled daily on TV. Miss Kitty had no time for Mr Coe's Method style of acting.

'Technique is the foundation on which all good acting is built,' she told Scarlett during one of her Saturday morning lessons. 'Bernard had marvellous technique *and* perfect posture. Sure, he could have been another Olivier – if he'd been a little taller. And no matter what your precious Mr Coe might say, no amount of *thinking himself tall* could make up the six inches that the good Lord chose to deny him.'

Miss Kitty talked a great deal about God – with whom she had regular communication – or *Him above* as she often said, while crossing herself. When Scarlett made the mistake of telling her that Mr Coe thought Shakespeare was God, Miss Kitty was understandably shocked.

Scarlett heartily wished she could have met the late, great Bernard. He sounded like a brilliant character, apparently given to wandering around the house learning his lines *in the altogether.*

'You mean *naked*?' Scarlett shrieked, scandalised.

'On these tiled floors! What are you thinking of, child?' said Miss Kitty. 'Sure, he always wore his slippers. One or two young actors were taken by surprise – when they came upon him unawares – but didn't they soon get used to him.'

As well as teaching, Miss Kitty also ran a boarding house for young actors performing at the local Civic Theatre. Scarlett was always hopeful that she would catch a glimpse of one of these magical creatures, but since her lesson was from ten until eleven o'clock on a Saturday morning, and the actors rarely rose before that time, she had strained in vain to see them.

Nevertheless, visiting Miss Kitty's house was always a thrill for Scarlett. She loved letting herself in through the big stained-glass front door; hearing her footsteps on the tiled mosaic hall floor; standing in the open stairwell where a sweeping staircase led up to five large bedrooms. She liked to imagine herself descending that staircase in a long flowing dress, making a stunning entrance, watched by an adoring crowd.

Scarlett's was the first lesson of the day and the silence in the house was broken only by the sound of clocks ticking and the low tones of the radio in the kitchen where Miss Kitty was usually to be found making coffee.

Scarlett had probably learned more about the glorious life of the theatre from Miss Kitty than the technical business of singing and voice. There *was* a lot of voice work in the lessons – although it was usually Miss Kitty's voice, with Scarlett doing the listening. But once they got underway, Kitty expected Scarlett to apply herself and work hard and long, her lessons often over-running by half an hour.

If ever Scarlett showed the slightest signs of fatigue Kitty would tell her, 'Oh, well, my dear, you might as well forget a career in the theatre. Acting requires a fierce commitment and a Herculean constitution.'

'Don't be thinking there's anything sissy about actors,' Kitty declared today. 'They're like athletes – immensely fit, and daring. Acting is not,' she warned Scarlett, 'for the faint-hearted.'

Miss Kitty was encouraging Scarlett to expand her lungs and extend her range. As an experiment she sent her out into the hallway and asked her to try to fill the space, challenging her to sing until her very lungs were bursting. Scarlett tried so hard she thought she might actually lose her voice, but the results barely made an impression in the huge space.

'You call that *loud*,' Miss Kitty said, witheringly. 'Open your mouth, child. From the bottom to the very top now, the full fine range. Free the Voice Beautiful. Let's lose those inhibitions!'

Scarlett was amused to think there was anyone who thought she still had inhibitions left to lose. Cleo often declared that Scarlett was born without any. She rose to Miss Kitty's challenge now, expanding her ribcage as instructed and concentrating on a spot in the near distance. She put so much energy into it that for a moment she felt dizzy, as if she might actually faint.

This time the sound seemed to spiral upwards through the stairwell and on up to the ceiling, and then began to echo in the most magical way. Scarlett could hardly believe *she* alone was making this glorious sound, but when she turned her eyes upwards she realised that she wasn't. Three of Miss Kitty's actors had come out of their rooms, still in their nightclothes, to join her. They seemed to be passing the notes between them like a party game.

Scarlett looked up at them in wonder as if, rather than humans, they were three of the angelic host of which Miss Kitty often spoke. When they stopped singing they gave Scarlett – and then one other – a round of applause before being sent off to their rooms like three naughty children.

'Now back to bed, my dears,' Kitty told them. 'Rest those precious voices.'

But before they did so they danced around the circular landing, laughing and waving to Scarlett. It was by far one of the most exciting things that had ever happened to her.

The rest of the lesson passed in a blur. It was only as she was leaving that Scarlett thought to ask Miss Kitty to wish her luck for her audition.

'Exactly what part would you be after?' she asked Scarlett.

'I'm hoping to get the main part – Othello,' Scarlett admitted.

Miss Kitty looked at her with her head on one side, her bird-like eyes fixed on Scarlett. She almost spoke, but then thought better of it and simply nodded.

'So you'll keep your fingers crossed for me?'

'Fingers crossed indeed! And what would be the point of that?' Kitty asked with a very serious face. But then she broke into a smile and added, 'Dear child, I shall be storming heaven with my prayers!'

When Scarlett got outside, Gemma was leaning on her bike waiting for her, as she often did after Scarlett's Saturday morning lesson.

'That was my best lesson *ever*!' Scarlett told Gemma. 'It...was...*doodylicious*!'

This was Scarlett's favourite word and the one she used when trying to describe the absolute heights of delight. In her excitement she was hopping from foot to foot. Scarlett described the whole experience in detail and only noticed that Gemma was silent and unmoved once she'd finished and was waiting in vain for some kind of response.

'Like hull-o-o,' she said, waving her hand in front of Gemma. 'Anyone at home?'

'Good for you,' was all Gemma said.

'What's wrong?'

'Nothing. I was just thinking how nice it must be having your own *private* lessons. *I* should be so lucky,' Gemma muttered miserably.

'I can't help it if...' unusually Scarlett was stuck for words, so Gemma finished her sentence for her, 'my mum and dad can afford to spoil me.'

'They don't *spoil* me,' Scarlett said, surprised.

'Not much,' said Gemma.

'Gemma...what is your problem?' Scarlett asked, sensing there was something more behind this.

'You've no idea, have you?' Gemma asked, getting on her bike and pedalling away.

'Where are you going?' Scarlett called after her.

But Gemma didn't even turn and look back.

Scarlett searched her brain for an explanation for

Gemma's increasingly odd behaviour. She could only think that it must be *hormonal*, which was how Scarlett had sometimes heard her mother explaining Cleo's frequent outbursts.

Trying to put it to the back of her mind, Scarlett returned instead to the much happier memory of *singing with the stars*, as she now liked to think of it.

Scarlett was so busy reliving the moment that she hardly noticed a bright blue sports car until it came to a stop beside her. A window opened and a hand emerged holding out a DVD. It was a film version of *Othello* and the hand belonged to Uncle Gerry. Scarlett took the DVD, and leaned inside the car to say hello.

'Just passed Gemma cycling in the other direction,' Gerry told Scarlett.

Scarlett pulled a face. 'She's got the hump with me for some reason. Actually, she's had the hump with me a lot lately.'

'What about?'

'I don't know. It seemed to be about me having singing lessons.'

'Sounds like the green-eyed monster,' said Gerry, pointing at the DVD.

Scarlett knew she'd heard the expression before.

'*It is the green-eyed monster which doth mock the meat it feeds on,*' Gerry recited. 'It's from *Othello*. I knew I'd got a copy somewhere. I watched a bit last night. It's very long – and over-acted – but you could fast-forward to the good bits. Want a lift home?'

Scarlett quickly got in the car and fastened her seat belt. She always felt cool riding in Gerry's car and wished her dad had one like it. Steve hadn't called for a couple of days and she suddenly experienced a rush of sadness just thinking about him. This had been one of his longest times away, nearly six weeks, and she really missed him.

'There're bound to be more recent versions of the play,' Gerry went on. 'You could look on the internet. This one's got Laurence Olivier playing *Othello* – blacked up! He looks absolutely ridiculous. It's almost from the dark ages – no pun intended.'

Scarlett studied the picture on the front. If Mr Coe gave Scarlett the part, instead of Leah, would he expect her to wear black make-up? Scarlett shrugged. She wouldn't like it, in fact she'd hate it, but an actress had to be able to deal with difficult situations. As Miss Kitty had said: acting was not for the faint-hearted.

*

When they arrived home Scarlett was keen to show Gerry how much her death scenes had improved. As usual, Gerry was enthusiastic, so much so that he challenged Scarlett to a contest. She could hardly contain her excitement.

They headed for the kitchen, where Scarlett's mum was busy emptying the dishwasher and making sandwiches for lunch. In addition she was now expected to act as audience and judge as Gerry and Scarlett prepared to *out-die* one another.

Scarlett went first, enthusiastically stabbing herself – on this occasion with a fish slice. She viciously stabbed three times, then recalling a line from *Julius Caesar*, gasped, 'Et tu, Brute? Then fall, Caesar!' and dropped to the floor with her usual flair.

'Bravo!' said Gerry, genuinely impressed.

Scarlett tried to look modest, but she knew that hers was a hard act to follow.

Gerry took a deep breath, thought for a moment, and chose poisoning.

Scarlett grinned excitedly as she watched him choke and splutter his way round the kitchen table, holding a bottle of soy sauce to his lips while clutching his stomach and groaning horribly. He finally succumbed, slumping onto the table, with a terrible gurgling noise that made Jenny burst out laughing.

Scarlett gave her mum a disapproving look. Dying was a serious business and she felt that laughter spoiled the effect. The soy sauce bottle was a nice touch and Scarlett made a mental note to copy it another time.

For her next attempt, Scarlett needed to come up with something entirely new. Inspired by Desdemona's death, she decided to smother herself – not an easy thing to do with an oven-glove. She struggled on, groaning and battling with it, until the oven-glove finally won and she died with a whimper, 'Oh, falsely, falsely murdered! Now, farewell!'

'Very touching,' Gerry said, brushing away a pretend tear or two and giving his nose a hearty blow. Scarlett smiled. She gave him a look that clearly said: follow that if you can.

For his finale Gerry chose the honourable way out – two fingers and a fist substituting for a gun, which he held to the side of his head. He blew out his brains, so effectively that Scarlett could almost imagine blood splattering the kitchen walls. She particularly admired the way Gerry slumped against the fridge then slid down to a sitting position on the kitchen floor, his eyes still wide open, staring as if he'd seen his own ghost. She burst into an enthusiastic bout of clapping.

'Who won? Who won?' she demanded of Mum, who judged it a draw. Scarlett and Gerry gave each other a big clap and retired to the kitchen table for tuna-mayo sandwiches.

Cleo stood in the doorway, rolling her eyes. 'I wish you wouldn't encourage her,' she told Gerry. 'We have to live with her, you know.'

Gerry just grinned and watched Scarlett attack the plate of sandwiches as if she hadn't eaten for a week. It would clearly take far more than a few gruesome death scenes to put Scarlett Lee off her food.

Chapter Four

Cake! Cake! My kingdom for some cake!

In her journal, Scarlett kept detailed notes on the different plays she was in. This was partly for her own benefit – to help her get things clearer in her mind. But she also liked to imagine some hopeful young actress coming to the same play in the future and having the advantage of Scarlett's insights and experience.

She turned to a new page and began, as she usually did, with a cast list.

OTHELLO – SCENES OF A BETRAYAL

CAST
Othello – The Moor of Venice and all-round good guy
Desdemona – Othello's young and beautiful wife

Iago – Othello's right-hand man
Emilia – Iago's wife
Cassio – Othello's second-in-command
Bianca – Cassio's mistress (!!!!)
Roderigo – Rich dude – fancies Desdemona
– bit of an idiot

It all starts off in Venice (a city that floats on water – I know all about that because I went there once). There's this guy called Othello who's a bit of a TOP BANANA. He wins all these battles and stuff. But he's not Italian, he's from North Africa, which makes him DIFFERENT!

Othello has a wife called Desdemona, who he sneaks off and marries in THE DEAD OF NIGHT. When people find out everyone seems fine about it, except Iago, for some reason. And Desdemona's father, who goes BALLISTIC!

Iago, Othello's right-hand man, decides to bring Othello down – APPARENTLY just because he's jealous of Othello. He's jealous of Cassio, too, because Othello's made him second-in-command and Iago wants the job. Iago is a real bad geezer and an out and out liar, but the man's got brains. He manages to persuade Othello that Desdemona and Cassio are having an AFFAIR. Othello goes MENTAL and has these fabuloso fainting fits.

In the end Othello tells Iago to kill Cassio. Then he goes to his own bedroom and smothers Desdemona. Not with kisses, with a pillow! Iago's wife, Emilia (who is also Desdemona's maid), comes in. She tells Othello it was all a big fat lie – he's been tricked. COINCIDENTALLY Iago comes in then and stabs Emilia to stop her from blabbing any more of the story. Then – COINCIDENTALLY again!! – a whole bunch of soldiers come in and arrest Othello and Iago. But Othello STABS himself in front of them all and dies slowly and dramatically – which is the best bit of the whole play!!!!

By the way, there's this other geezer called Roderigo who's a bit of an idiot, but he's a rich idiot. He wanted to marry Desdemona, *too, and Iago uses him to cause BIG trouble between Othello and Cassio.*

Sooo...in the end, Desdemona's dead on the bed; Emilia's dead by her side; Othello falls dead on top of them. Wicked!

Scarlett was pleased to have remembered so much of the story, but then she had spent Sunday morning watching Uncle Gerry's DVD. He'd been right about it being miles too long, though, and she'd fast-forwarded a lot of it. In the end Scarlett hadn't been too impressed.

Miss Kitty says Laurence Olivier was probably our GREATEST STAGE ACTOR EVER, but I would only give this film two out of ten. It was too long, everyone shouted all the time in posh accents and Laurence Olivier was covered in what looked like brown boot polish, which was A VERY BAD IDEA! Every time he kissed Desdemona I thought it would rub off on her face.

Death scenes: four out of ten. I could definitely have done better.

But the chance to stab herself in front of an audience wasn't the only reason Scarlett was keen to play Othello. When Mr Coe had described him as a noble and heroic character, possibly Shakespeare's most romantic hero, Scarlett had thought that really the part could have been written for her.

She did briefly think that playing Desdemona might be fun, too. She was sure she could do *being smothered*, just as well as *being stabbed*. She put her journal aside and briefly lay on her bed practising with a pillow, until she got too hot and had to come up for air.

Scarlett wouldn't even have minded playing Roderigo, who was a bit of a clown, because Mr Coe had once told Scarlett that she had excellent comic timing. She'd been playing an old man with a walking stick and a wig at the time and developed such a funny walk that the other girls hadn't been able to deliver their lines and Mr Coe had had to remind them that comedy only works when the actors stay in character and leave the audience to do the laughing.

But Scarlett had really set her heart on playing Othello and she was pretty confident she'd get it. In fact, she'd been busy most of the weekend doing what Mr Coe called *learning to inhabit* the part. This involved wandering round the house wearing an old velvet curtain, behaving like royalty and expecting her mum and Cleo to treat her as such. Whenever they didn't, she glared haughtily at them, although disappointingly they didn't always notice.

Cleo did notice, though, that when Sunday lunch was over Scarlett made a stately exit, leaving the *'servants'* to do the clearing up. Cleo complained bitterly to their mum about *some people having delusions of grandeur.*

Back in her bedroom, Sunday afternoon hung heavily for Scarlett. Two or three times over the weekend she'd texted Gemma, with no response. She finally called the house phone, in case Gemma's mobile was dead. Gemma's mum answered and, after calling upstairs, told Scarlett that Gemma wasn't there. But Scarlett knew better. She had clearly heard Gemma saying, 'I'm not talking to her.'

To cheer herself up, Scarlett decided to do some

mirror work. She began with a few facial exercises, screwing up her nose and circling it round her face. Initially this always made her giggle because she looked exactly like a rabbit, but, once she was nicely warmed up, Scarlett settled down to practise different expressions.

For homework Miss Kitty had suggested that Scarlett try acting entirely with her eyes. She tried: *surprised...scared...disgusted...disappointed...bored ...angry...*

In fact, Scarlett was so engrossed that she didn't notice the door opening and Cleo putting her head round it. When she finally did, she braced herself for one of her sister's scathing remarks, but instead Cleo said quietly, and rather ominously, 'You'd better come down. Dad's on the phone.'

Although Scarlett wouldn't really admit to having a nervous bone in her body, the look on Cleo's face suggested that she might need to prepare herself for trouble. Scarlett arranged her face into a suitably serious expression and reached for her hairbrush. She began brushing vigorously.

It was a harmless habit that most people assumed was vanity. Other girls bit their nails, chewed their lips, or still sucked their thumbs, but at times of stress Scarlett brushed her hair – until it crackled.

The three of them sat around the living room, each with a phone in her hand. There was definitely an atmosphere and Scarlett felt as if she'd arrived late to a play and missed an important bit of the plot. But there was no time to find out what before Dad asked, 'So, how's the play going?'

Scarlett began a blow-by-blow account of her preparations for the audition but had barely got into her stride before Mum interrupted.

'Steve, I think you should just get on and tell the girls.' She turned to them, 'Dad's got some news.'

Scarlett glanced at Cleo, who shrugged; she didn't seem to know what this was about either.

'Da-a-ad, what's going on?' Scarlett asked nervously.

'It's nothing. Nothing for you to worry about anyway,' he reassured her. 'Nothing at all.'

'Steve!' Jenny pressed him again.

'OK. Well, it's *good* news. Guess who's got the chance to go on a sailing trip?' No one answered so Steve pressed on. 'Phil Slattery's asked me to help him sail his new yacht across to the States.'

Phil Slattery was one of their dad's business clients – the wealthiest – the one the girls had nicknamed *Slottery Ticket*. They both showed signs of relief now: surely that was good news? So what was Mum's long face about?

'When?' Cleo asked.

'Leaving this week.'

'Day after tomorrow!' Mum added.

'Wow! That's soon,' said Scarlett.

'Why haven't you told us before?' Cleo asked. She could sense there was more to come.

'I've only known for a week or so, it wasn't settled...it still isn't,' Dad hastened to add. 'If you all tell me you don't want me to go, I won't go, it's as simple as that.'

Scarlett glanced at her mum, then at Cleo. This was like her dad's biggest dream come true. They could all hear the excitement in his voice. They wanted him home, especially Scarlett, but how could they possibly tell him he couldn't go?

There was a long pause in which no one spoke; they were all wrestling with their feelings, waiting for someone else to break the silence.

'Hello! Are you still there?' their dad asked.

'Yes,' said Mum. 'We're still here.' She opened her hands and gestured to the girls: it was up to them to speak now.

'It'll be great, Dad,' Cleo said, trying to sound as if she meant it. 'You'll still be able to phone us, won't you?'

'Of course,' Steve reassured them. 'Maybe not quite so often.'

'So how long's it going to take?' Scarlett suddenly thought to ask.

She could almost hear her dad draw breath before he replied, 'Six weeks...maybe a bit less.'

'Six weeks!!!' Scarlett screamed. '*Six weeks there and six weeks back*?!!'

She was so loud that her mum and Cleo both let go of the phones and covered their ears.

'No, no, I'll be flying home from the States. It won't take more than six weeks altogether, I promise.'

Scarlett wanted to remind her dad that he'd been away that long already. This would make it the longest time they'd ever been without him. She was *desperate* to have him home...and, of course, there was the small matter of her play...

'Oh, Dad, that means...' Scarlett began.

But Cleo narrowed her eyes and silently mouthed,

'*Don't* even say it,' so Scarlett had to swallow the words and turn it into some bit of nonsense.

Dad promised to email them with an itinerary of the places he'd be stopping at on the way. He mentioned a few and everyone listened, making polite and encouraging noises, but their faces told a very different story.

After the phone call was finished, they each sat there for a few minutes with their own thoughts. Inside, Scarlett was battling with a deep sense of how unfair life was, especially for her, but one look at her mum's face told her she'd better *keep* it inside. Instead Scarlett reached for the comfort of her hairbrush, only to find it had disappeared.

'You want to be careful,' Cleo warned her. 'All that brushing – your hair might fall out, and then who's going to want a *bald* actress?'

Scarlett was already in a bad mood, and when the hairbrush turned up later – behind the cushion Cleo had been leaning against – she flew into a fury. Their mum could see where things were heading.

'I don't know about you two, but I need a hug,' she said, sitting in the middle of the sofa and opening her arms wide. The girls stopped fighting and went to sit beside her. She hugged them closely.

'Listen, none of us wants Dad to go on this trip, do we?'

Both girls shook their heads sadly.

'But we're not going to tell Dad that, are we?'

Again the girls gave a resigned shake of their heads.

'This is going to be a difficult six weeks for us girls. So what do we need to do?'

'Stick together,' said Scarlett miserably.

'That's right,' said Mum. 'And when the going gets tough, what do the tough do?'

'Get baking!' the girls shouted in unison, jumping up and heading into the kitchen.

Ever since Scarlett could remember Mum had used baking as a way to cheer everyone up when things got difficult. It seemed the perfect answer to Scarlett: you got the fun of baking and then something scrummy to eat at the end of it.

Mum pushed a recipe book towards Cleo and an apron in Scarlett's direction. She pulled out a mixing bowl, and a bag of flour from the food cupboard.

'So, what's it to be?'

'Cake! Cake! My kingdom for some cake!' Scarlett

declared, wearing the apron and brandishing a large wooden spoon.

Cleo rolled her eyes, but Mum smiled in her direction.

'OK, Cleo, you get to choose what kind.'

While they baked they started to get their heads around the news. Everyone agreed that Dad deserved this trip. Even with all her disappointment Scarlett couldn't deny that fact. Her father was a great dad – easy-going, big and dependable, like a rock. He worked really hard, sometimes late into the night, but he was never too busy if the girls needed him.

Cleo would miss him because he was her best ally on the conservation campaign. They would talk for hours about her latest discoveries, and the different ways in which they might help to save the planet between them.

But Scarlett felt sure she missed her dad more. Even now she still occasionally liked nothing better than to snuggle up on his knee while he tested her on her lines. She liked to think of her dad as a big cuddly bear and her mum as a little one. She and Cleo sometimes called their mum and dad *Little and Large*. In fact, Jenny was so tiny she often complained she had only to look at a cream cake and she'd be shopping for the next size.

But for now putting on weight wasn't uppermost on anyone's mind. The three of them sat on the sofa, each with a big fat slice of orange drizzle cake, trying to decide which DVD to watch.

'I wouldn't mind watching *Othello* again,' Scarlett suggested helpfully.

'Well, I *would*,' Cleo snorted. 'I want cheering up, not boring out of my brain.'

'I know,' said Mum, and her smile gave Scarlett the clue. She jumped up and took *Titanic* out of the rack. It was one of their favourites. They all leaned back in happy anticipation as the opening credits rolled. Scarlett sang her way through most of the soundtrack, to Cleo's disgust.

When it was finished, however, even Scarlett wondered if it had been the best choice. Considering the trip their dad was about to make, the fact that the *Titanic* sinks and most of the passengers perish felt like it could have been a bad omen. But no one wanted to think about that.

Instead their mum looked down at her plate and sighed. 'Oh dear. By the time Dad comes home I shall be the size of a small house.'

The girls gave her a quick cuddle and told her that their dad would still love her anyway.

Despite the fact that their family was often physically separated, Cleo and Scarlett knew that they were lucky to have a mum and dad still together. Lots of their friends' parents had split up and remarried. But their parents were like two pieces of furniture; it was inconceivable that anyone would ever split *them* up. It was probably the thing that made it all bearable, for Scarlett at least. As she was quick to reassure her mum, 'Dad'd still love you if you were the size of a block of flats!'

'Thanks, Scarlett,' her mum frowned. 'Cheer me up, why don't you.'

Chapter Five

No small parts – only small actors!

Scarlett had little time over the next couple of days to feel depressed about her dad's news, because there was still so much work to do on her audition piece. And Scarlett felt she had had to do most of that work on her own, because Gemma seemed reluctant to even meet up. The whole weekend had passed without the girls even talking on the phone.

They had finally managed one rushed rehearsal on Monday lunchtime that hadn't improved relations between them, although Scarlett had been too wrapped up in her own performance to notice very much.

When Gemma, looking for a little reassurance, had asked Scarlett, 'How do you think I'm doing? Do you think I'll get the part?'

Scarlett had sighed, 'Yeah, yeah, whatever.'

She hadn't even glanced up from her script, or she might have seen the look on Gemma's face – the look that clearly showed this was the straw that finally broke the camel's back.

Suddenly it was Tuesday, Drama Club day, and the auditions were upon them. Scarlett had woken that morning to a room she'd filled with positive messages for herself. This was another of Miss Kitty's practical suggestions. Messages like: *I was born to play Othello! This part is mine! No one could do it better! Today is the first day of the rest of my brilliant career!*

Scarlett went off to school feeling upbeat, almost carefree. The mood lasted throughout the day, despite her worries about her dad and Gemma's continuing coolness towards her. She still had no idea what that was about!

After school everyone collected in the Drama Club cloakroom amid a cloud of nervous anticipation, waiting for Mr Coe to arrive.

The only disadvantage to the building, the girls generally agreed, was in fact the scruffy cloakroom, with its poor lighting and cracked mirror. But despite this handicap they were all managing to apply make-up and arrange their hairstyles in ways that wouldn't have been allowed during regular school hours. Apart that is from Brogan, who scorned what she called *girly stuff*. She sat on a bench in the corner puffing out her cheeks and jiggling her legs while the rest got ready and compared how nervous they were feeling.

Not for the first time Scarlett felt thankful *she* wasn't a martyr to nerves. After a quick toss of her hair and a pinch of her cheeks – something she'd seen Scarlett O'Hara do in *Gone with the Wind* – Scarlett sat beside Brogan, having a last look at her lines.

Gemma came to sit beside Scarlett; they were still speaking, but only just. Scarlett tried to cheer Gemma up in her usual tried and tested way, with a few more impressions: Minnie with her habitual sniff, Rhiannon raising her eyebrows and looking north to north-east whenever someone said something she didn't entirely believe, and shy, nervous Priya chewing the inside of her cheeks with concentration.

Gemma hardly cracked a smile and finally Scarlett gave up. She was beginning to find it all a bit of a drag. Gemma could be a bit sulky at times and that was something she found less than endearing about her friend. Scarlett wished Gemma would hurry up and get over herself.

'Are you feeling OK, Gemma?' Brogan asked her, not too helpfully. 'You've gone an awfully weird colour.'

Gemma had no time to reply before the girls heard Mr Coe arriving. They all got to their feet and went off to meet their fates. Scarlett noticed for the first time how very pale Gemma was looking.

'Just remember to take deep breaths,' she tried to reassure her friend. 'You'll be fine.' Scarlett gave her hair a few quick brushstrokes and added, 'Keep your fingers crossed for me.'

'If you'll keep yours crossed for me,' Gemma answered pointedly.

'Yeah, 'course,' Scarlett quickly replied, although she'd forgotten for the moment exactly which part it was Gemma was after.

Mr Coe began with his usual little pep talk. He reminded them that nerves were entirely a point of view. The girls could call it *stage fright* and choose to work themselves up into a frenzy so that they couldn't even deliver their lines – or they could call it *excitement*: energy just waiting to be released. It was really up to them.

Scarlett beamed at Mr Coe, almost nodding in her enthusiasm. It was a similar message to the one Miss Kitty had given her before her Speech and Drama exam. 'Think of yourself going down a slide into a swimming pool,' Miss Kitty had advised. 'Don't be holding onto yourself like you're going to your death, muttering, *Oh, God! Oh, God!* Throw your arms wide to the heavens and shout, *Oh, joy! Oh, joy!*'

Scarlett whispered a few *oh joys* now under her breath. Then, ignoring Gemma's horrified look, she volunteered them to go first.

Mr Coe had a typically unconventional approach to auditions. He didn't insist the girls choose a piece from the play they were auditioning for. Instead he encouraged each of them to choose their own piece – something which would show each of them off to their best advantage.

Scarlett had thought carefully about the suitability of her and Gemma's audition piece. She'd chosen a short scene from *Macbeth*, a play that, like *Othello*, had more than its fair share of tragedy and provided lots of dramatic moments.

Despite Gemma's nerves, as far as Scarlett could tell it all went pretty well. She was a little disappointed, though, when Mr Coe asked her to hurry along at one point because he had a lot more people to get through that day.

Scarlett and Gemma were now free to sit back while the others did their pieces, Scarlett keeping up a running commentary on how each of them performed.

Zara did her usual monologue from *Annie*. She had once auditioned for a part in the chorus of the local Amateur Dramatic Society production and ever since she'd talked as though it had been her ten minutes of fame – even though she'd never actually got a part.

'Big mistake,' was Scarlett's verdict. 'Five out of ten. Seen it all before.' Which to be fair they had.

Brogan, who always liked playing the clown, did a short scene she'd improvised about a man working in a fish and chip shop. Showing off to the customers, he tosses the fish in the air and when it falls it hits him on the head and knocks him out. It was a great piece of slapstick and had everyone, including Mr Coe, helpless with laughter.

Scarlett awarded it eight out of ten, but added, 'Do you think she's forgotten it's a tragedy we're auditioning for?'

Apparently this hadn't occurred to most of the other girls either. Leah did a song and dance routine from *Joseph and the Amazing Technicolor Dreamcoat.*

'Not bad, the girl can dance,' said Scarlett, awarding another eight.

Abbie did a monologue from *The Worst Witch* that impressed Scarlett so much she gave her nine out of ten. Abbie always gave everything a hundred and ten per cent and Scarlett might have given her a ten, if she hadn't tripped over her cloak on leaving the stage.

After all the other girls had performed, Eve, the new girl, went last, surprising everyone with a very good excerpt from a traditional story about a young girl who gets lost in a wood at night and ends up being poisoned by an apple given to her by an old woman – who was clearly a witch. She forgot one or two of her lines, but Scarlett was still a little envious of how well she died. She raised her eyebrows and whispered to Gemma, 'Who's the dark horse, then?'

Mr Coe gave them a ten-minute break while he read through his notes – then they reconvened to hear his verdict. The girls noisily filed back into the room, Scarlett feeling quietly confident.

Mr Coe was generally very popular with the girls, but

there were a couple of ways in which they sometimes found him frustrating. For instance, he never felt obliged to follow his own rules. He talked a lot about democracy; about everyone having a voice; about everyone's opinion being valued. But in the end the girls couldn't help noticing that it was always Mr Coe who had the casting vote. They often suspected he'd made up his mind before they'd even auditioned.

Today the teacher began by asking each of the girls which part she would *like* to play and which part she felt suited to. This proved to be inconclusive since almost everyone wanted to play Othello and felt they would be perfectly well-suited to the role. Scarlett hadn't expected so much competition and was glad she hadn't confided in the other girls, so that when Mr Coe got round to her she could reply, 'Oh, I really don't mind. Whatever you think, Mr Coe.'

Gemma flashed her a look, but Scarlett glanced away innocently.

Mr Coe then gave them all another familiar pep talk about acting being first and foremost teamwork. He reminded them yet again that, in the words of the great Stanislavski, *there were no small parts – only small actors.*

But today Mr Coe had added a new theme – that acting was a journey of self-discovery. He wanted to encourage the girls to come right out of their comfort zones and act against type. In fact his main aim for this production was for the girls to explore a completely new side to themselves.

The girls weren't sure what this meant, but they didn't like the sound of it. They were not in the least reassured when he gave the first part – of Desdemona – to Brogan! In fact there was an uprising, led by Brogan, who almost bellowed at him, 'You have got to be joking, Mr C!'

Scarlett couldn't agree more, but Mr Coe smiled and quietly insisted that he was certainly not joking. He pressed on and gave Gemma – not in anyone's eyes a natural comic – the part of Roderigo. Zara, who usually got the beautiful heroines, but in Scarlett's view was always playing *Annie*, was given Bianca.

Zara wasn't stupid. Even though Mr Coe kept describing Bianca as Cassio's *girlfriend*, she knew the difference between a girlfriend and a mistress! Zara felt insulted and pressed her perfect lips angrily together.

One by one all the parts were allocated: Abbie was

given Emilia, Iago's wife, and Leah got Cassio. This pleased Leah, who seemed quite happy to be playing what she called *the lurve interest*, and Scarlett, who was delighted that her main competition for Othello had been eliminated.

Minnie, Priya and Rhiannon shared the minor characters between them, until finally only the two main characters remained. Scarlett felt secretly delighted that her strategy had paid off. She was a little surprised that the new girl, Eve, was going to get Iago, but Mr Coe must have his reasons.

The teacher went on to explain that the play, despite its title, was really Iago's: his was the more challenging, and probably more important part. This came as something of a surprise to Scarlett, but she felt confident that her Othello would prove Mr Coe wrong. Hadn't she once while still at infant school stolen a whole Christmas show when she played a snowflake with only one line to deliver?

Scarlett stopped daydreaming and pricked up her ears when she heard her name mentioned.

'Surely, Mr Coe, if Iago is *such* a difficult and important part, Scarlett should play him,' Gemma suggested. 'Everyone know she's the best.'

Scarlett stared in disbelief at Gemma, who refused to catch her eye. Instead she kept on gazing at Mr Coe with an innocent look on her face.

'Well, Gemma, I must agree with you. Scarlett often plays the hero, but this time I want Eve to try *Othello*. Let's see what kind of a villain Scarlett can make.'

No one was more surprised than Eve, who gave a little gasp before turning bright pink. Scarlett's mouth was opening and closing as she searched for the right thing to say – and how to say it – without completely losing her cool.

Immediately the other girls were clamouring for Mr Coe's attention. They had a long list of complaints and questions, not least of all what Mr Coe proposed to do about the fact that Othello was meant to be black; Eve was the palest of them all, with almost white-blonde hair.

Mr Coe agreed that Eve didn't on the surface look the part, but he wasn't interested in that. He told them that, in fact, critics were divided over the question of Othello's colour. The Moors, sometimes called Berbers, came from North Africa, he said, and had light tawny skin. But he didn't want them to dwell on Othello's skin colour. He wanted them to think of him simply as an outsider, a foreigner, *not one of them*. Probably, as the newest girl to the school, Eve would have some valuable experience to bring to the part.

Scarlett stayed absolutely silent. She was trying to make sense of what had just occurred, but her brain somehow wouldn't compute it. She couldn't wait for the session to finish so that she could confront Gemma. She caught up with her outside in the corridor, grabbing her arm as Gemma quickly headed off.

'I thought you were my friend,' she said.

'Yes, well, I thought *you* were *my* friend,' Gemma replied coolly.

Scarlett couldn't understand what that was supposed to mean.

'I thought you were my *best* friend,' she tried again.

'You *know* I'm your best friend,' Gemma continued, confusingly.

'So – if you're supposed to be my best friend – why did you do that?'

'Do what?' Gemma asked.

'Set me up like that.'

Gemma shrugged. 'I only told the truth. You heard Mr Coe; you've got the main part, which was what you wanted.'

'I *wanted* Othello,' Scarlett moaned.

'I *wanted* Desdemona,' said Gemma. 'We don't always get what we want. Welcome to the real world.' And Gemma walked off down the corridor, leaving Scarlett more confused than ever.

Scarlett walked home alone still trying to make sense of things. She couldn't believe that Gemma, of all people, had done this. *She knew how much I wanted it,* kept running through Scarlett's brain.

Scarlett had been so sure she was going to get the part, too. She felt like someone who'd been promised (well, not *exactly* promised) a big fat ice cream, only to have it snatched away and offered to someone else. She couldn't wait to get home to a sympathetic audience.

As Scarlett walked back to the house she was preparing her opening lines: *You are* never *going to believe what's just happened...* She even planned her moves – throwing down her bag dramatically, closing her eyes, maybe clenching her fists, taking a long deep breath and then spilling the whole story: the lead-up, their brilliant audition piece, her patient wait while the minor parts were given out, and then – the climax

of her story – the ambush, the knife in the back...
the betrayal.

Scarlett felt completely cheated, which she thought put her in a very positive light. Her family were bound to be outraged on her behalf. She walked a little faster to get the news to them as soon as she could.

As she turned the corner of her street, Scarlett was surprised to see a police car parked outside her house.

Hmm! She was suddenly torn between a sense of frustration that this would delay her telling her story, and curiosity about what the police could possibly be doing there.

She would have to save her performance as poor, put-upon victim for later. After all, she thought as she crossed the street, if she was going to be stuck with the role of the villain, who better to assist her in her research than the police! She might even get their professional opinion on her death scenes. Policemen were bound to have seen lots of people dying, she thought.

Never one to waste an opportunity, Scarlett hurried through the back door in a much more positive frame of mind.

Chapter Six

This was the most unkindest cut...

Scarlett dumped her bag in the kitchen and headed for the lounge, where she could see her mum standing, talking to two policemen.

Unfortunately, Cleo was blocking the doorway.

'What's going on?' Scarlett hissed in her sister's ear. Cleo flinched and didn't answer, but made room for Scarlett to pass.

'This is my younger daughter,' their mum introduced her. 'Scarlett, this is DI Maddox and PC Dryer.'

The older man, who wasn't wearing a uniform, was heavily built. His hair was beginning to thin on top, like Mr Coe's, and he looked, to Scarlett, as if he spent too much time sitting at a desk, eating takeaways out of foil containers. His face was heavy too and a bit morose, but it changed completely when he smiled and Scarlett took an instant liking to him.

The younger policeman was very tall and thin and he hunched his shoulders as if trying to take up less space. He seemed too shy to actually smile at her, and only managed a nod instead.

Scarlett beamed back at them, excitedly. She was bursting to ask what they'd come for; what they could tell her about villains; and would they like to see her die? But the moment she opened her mouth, Cleo stood on her foot.

'Ow! What was that for?'

'Girls, kitchen!' their mum said, pointing the way.

'What's going on?' Scarlett asked the moment they were out of earshot.

'It's some rubbish about vandalism around Dad's office. Nothing you'd be interested in,' Cleo told her.

'Boring,' Scarlett agreed.

'Mum's told them he's out of the country and can't help but they don't seem to want to go away. Now they're quizzing her about his number plates, like they're trying to find something to pick on.'

'Number plates?' Scarlett screwed up her nose.

'They must have spotted them when they walked up the drive.'

The phone rang and the girls heard their mum pick it up.

'You'd think they'd have better things to do with their time,' Cleo was still complaining as the two policemen appeared in the kitchen. The older one, DI Maddox, smiled pleasantly at her. 'Your mum's busy on the phone,' he explained.

Cleo, determined *she* wasn't going to chat to them, narrowed her eyes and looked away, but Scarlett simply couldn't help herself.

'Are you going to send Dad to prison?' she asked.

'Why, has he broken the law?'

''Cause of his number plates.'

'Probably not this time, not for a first offence,' DI Maddox replied, smiling.

'Do you want to watch me die?' Scarlett asked, putting down her drink and, without waiting for a reply, throwing herself dramatically to the floor.

'Good God,' said DI Maddox, rushing round the kitchen table. He stared down at Scarlett, seriously concerned. 'Is she all right?'

'No, she's only got half a brain,' said Cleo, 'but

she'll live, *unfortunately*. Get up and stop acting the fool,' she told Scarlett.

Scarlett reluctantly got up and dusted her clothes down. 'In your professional opinion,' she asked, 'how convincing would you say that was? On a scale of one to ten?'

'Well, it scared the life out of me,' he said, 'so I'd say it rated a nine at least.'

Scarlett was most gratified. 'Would you like a cup of tea?' she asked.

Cleo sighed heavily, but DI Maddox pretended not to notice.

'How very kind,' he replied, immediately seating himself at the kitchen table. 'Milk, no sugar for me,' he added, 'and three sugars for the growing lad.'

'Surely he's not going to grow any more?' Scarlett asked, studying the young man critically. 'He's enormous already. But I suppose that's quite useful if you're a police officer.'

PC Dryer hovered awkwardly in the doorway, glancing shyly at Cleo, who glared back at him, while Scarlett and the detective continued to discuss him as if he wasn't there.

'He's a bit shy around girls,' DI Maddox confided,

'especially pretty ones like you and your sister.'

'Oh, he needn't be shy of us. I'm too young for him and Cleo's finished with boys. She says they're as much use as a chocolate teapot.'

Cleo hissed warningly at Scarlett.

'Well, that's what you said.' Scarlett, embarrassed by Cleo's coldness, gave PC Dryer a friendly smile to compensate.

If Cleo hadn't been there, Scarlett would have gone on to explain that since the beginning of the year Cleo had been dumped by four boyfriends in quick succession, more than average bad luck by anyone's standards. Cleo had sworn never to go out with anyone again and instead committed herself exclusively to the cause of conservation.

'This is a very nice house,' DI Maddox said, looking round him. 'I suppose you must have a place in Spain as well, with your dad working out there?'

'Oh, no, Dad just rents an office with a room over it,' Scarlett told him. 'He will buy a place though, when he's very rich.'

Cleo glared at Scarlett, who knew quite well what that look meant: *don't tell everyone our business*. Scarlett ignored her and handed the two policemen cups of tea, then infuriated Cleo even further by offering them the last two pieces of orange drizzle cake. DI Maddox took one but the young policeman refused.

'Have you had a lot of experience with villains?' Scarlett asked next.

'It sort of goes with the job,' DI Maddox replied, smiling, and making short work of the cake.

'No, I mean, *real* villains. You know, *evil* types. I'm trying to find out what makes them tick.'

'Well, now,' DI Maddox replied, 'even in our line of work, you don't come across real evil every day. Mostly we deal with the unfortunates, the inadequates, the drunk and the stupid. Real evil's pretty rare.'

Scarlett was a little disappointed. 'I was hoping you could give me some inside information,' she said.

'I hope you're not planning a life of crime,' he smiled.

Scarlett sensed she was being teased. 'Actually, it's research for a part I'm playing in the school play – *Othello*.'

DI Maddox looked impressed, but just then Scarlett's mum came into the kitchen. 'I'm sorry, that was my husband ringing. I told him why you were here, but he couldn't help. As I said, he's been out of the country for over a month.'

'Dad?!' Scarlett squealed. 'Why didn't you tell me, so I could say goodbye?'

'Is your husband going somewhere?' DI Maddox asked pleasantly.

'He's about to sail across the Atlantic,' Mum replied.

'Is he now? And how long will that take?'

'Six weeks or more.'

'Not *more*,' Scarlett corrected her mum. 'He promised it wouldn't be *more* than six weeks.'

'He must have a big boat for that kind of trip?'

'It's not *his* boat,' Scarlett answered. 'It's Slottery Ticket's. But he is going to have his own – one day.'

Mum shook her head as if to say, *don't mind Scarlett.* 'The boat belongs to one of his clients,' she explained. 'My husband's going along as part of the crew.'

Scarlett could tell that her mum was getting weary of all these questions, but was trying to be polite. She looked as if she'd be glad when they went away and left her in peace.

When DI Maddox said, 'That was a very delicious cup of tea your daughter made us. I don't suppose there's any left in the pot?' Scarlett saw her mum's shoulders sag, before reluctantly filling the kettle for a second round of tea.

Cleo glared hard at Scarlett, who glared back. It was hardly her fault!

Half an hour later, as the policemen were driving away, Gerry's car drew up outside. Even though she was usually glad to see him, Scarlett's mum sighed again as if any new visitor was one too many.

'No one's asked me about any vandalism,' Gerry said, surprised when he'd heard about the policemen's visit. 'It's a wonder the police have got two hours to waste on such trivial business.'

'And then they got started on Steve's number plates,' Jenny added. 'I've warned him about those before.'

Scarlett's dad had found the perfect number plates on the internet: STE 31Y, which at a glance – because of the way he'd had them printed – spelled out Steely, his nickname from his schooldays.

'Loads of people have personalised number plates,' Cleo chipped in.

'But they're not *strictly* legal,' her mum pointed out. 'Apparently because of the way they're run together.'

'It's hardly a serious business, though,' Gerry said. 'I've a good mind to get onto the local station and complain.'

'Don't bother,' said Jenny. 'I'm sure they're only doing their job. But I did wonder when they were ever going to leave.'

'We all know whose fault that was,' Cleo said pointedly.

'You can't blame me,' said Scarlett. 'I think it was all just an excuse for that young one to make eyes at you.' She did a brilliant imitation of the young policeman shooting sidelong looks at Cleo, and clutching his heart. Gerry burst out laughing, and their mum reached out an arm to restrain Cleo before she made a lunge at Scarlett.

'How about I go and get us a takeaway?' Gerry suggested. He could see how tired and flat the whole family was looking. 'My treat,' he added.

No one took much persuading.

'Doodylicious!' Scarlett declared.

'Anyone coming for the ride?' Gerry asked.

'Me, me, me!' Scarlett jumped up.

'Yes, take her, please,' Cleo begged. 'At least it will give us a few minutes' peace.'

*

In the car, Gerry asked Scarlett what kind of a day she'd had. Scarlett suddenly realised that she hadn't yet had a chance to tell anyone about her big disappointment! Now the floodgates opened and she let it all pour out.

'The thing is...' Scarlett went on, encouraged by Gerry's sympathetic noises, 'I was going to be brilliant in the death scene. I've practised stabbing myself so many times. And my fainting fits would have been a-*mazing*. Instead I'm stuck with Iago, who doesn't even get to die, for goodness' sake! He just runs off, which is *pathetic*!'

Scarlett was especially disappointed that, as Iago, she wouldn't even get to enjoy being tortured, because that didn't happen until after the play was over. What a waste of her impressive range of moans, groans and blood-curdling screams, she thought.

'Well, Iago may not be the part you wanted,' Gerry consoled her, 'but it's a *big* part and a real challenge. And in the end you know you'll steal the show, like you always do, so it really doesn't matter.'

Scarlett smiled, pacified at last. She sat up a little

taller in her seat. Uncle Gerry always had a knack for making her feel better. Maybe he and Mr Coe were right: she was ready for this challenge.

But it still seemed a pity about the torture. Such a waste, she thought.

Chapter Seven

Now is the winter of our discontent...

By Saturday morning, although Scarlett hadn't quite got over her sense of disappointment, she was beginning to get used to the two new realities: that her dad would be away for what felt like half a lifetime, and that her dreams of playing *Othello* had been well and truly shattered.

As she walked to her lesson with Miss Kitty, Scarlett knew that she would need to put a brave face on things. Her singing teacher expected a stiff upper lip in these situations.

'Never show your disappointment,' she always impressed upon Scarlett. 'Remember – gracious in defeat.'

Nevertheless, Scarlett was impatient to tell Miss Kitty her audition result and perhaps get some words of sympathy and understanding. So she was a little surprised to hear a lesson already in progress when she arrived; Miss Kitty must have a new pupil. There was a note taped to the studio door asking Scarlett to wait in the kitchen and to help herself to a drink.

Scarlett didn't need a drink. She always carried a bottle of water wherever she went because Miss Kitty had impressed on her the importance of keeping her system hydrated. It was tap water, of course – bottled water being a wicked waste of the world's resources and strictly banned by Cleo.

She wandered into the kitchen and spent the time studying the photos that covered the kitchen walls, imagining her own having pride of place there one day. Many were of young actors that had spent time boarding with Kitty. None as far as Scarlett knew were exactly famous, but they were all *serious* actors. Every one of them, Kitty assured her, would've taken poison before allowing themselves to appear on a reality TV show.

Nor would Scarlett ever dream of doing anything like that! She shared her teacher's disdain for people who wanted fame for its own sake, regardless of whether they had any talent.

There were plenty of photos of Bernard in various plays by Shakespeare. He'd never taken the lead exactly, but he had played many minor characters to great acclaim, according to Miss Kitty.

Before Bernard, Miss Kitty had been married twice: first to a missionary with whom she had travelled throughout Africa and who had died quite young, and then to a much older and richer man who'd also died. From him she'd inherited the family fortune, including her large Victorian house. Finally, she'd met Bernard – the love of her life – and been idyllically happy *until his Maker had carried him off*, as Kitty described it.

Scarlett went on to read the menus for the coming week. Miss Kitty provided meals for the actors, or *her children*, as she liked to refer to them. She often despaired of the way young actors mistreated their bodies and warned Scarlett about the five deadly sins: smoking, drinking, drugs, staying up all night and eating erratically. She could at least make sure that her actors had one good meal a day inside them. Tonight, Scarlett read, it was chilli bean casserole. Scarlett groaned out loud. She hoped that as an actress she would never have to become a vegetarian.

Just the thought of red kidney beans made Scarlett shudder!

Scarlett assumed this menu meant that the actors must still be in rehearsal. Miss Kitty had told Scarlett that once the actual performances began she had to be careful not to feed them *fart-food*. One of the things Scarlett loved about Miss Kitty was that, unlike most adults she knew, Kitty never minced her words.

At last Scarlett heard the studio door open. She hurried out into the hall, more than a little curious to get a glimpse of Miss Kitty's new pupil. Scarlett felt quite territorial around her teacher. She knew it was silly; Miss Kitty taught lots of other pupils, but she liked to think that they had a special relationship.

Imagine Scarlett's surprise when she walked straight into the mysterious new pupil and discovered that it was...Gemma!

The two girls hastily stepped back and stared at one another, but neither spoke. It wasn't a surprise for Gemma; she knew the time of Scarlett's lesson. She looked down a little shamefacedly, but Scarlett couldn't stop staring at her.

'You never said you were starting lessons,' she said, in an accusing tone.

'You never asked,' Gemma replied. She thanked Miss Kitty and walked out.

Miss Kitty smiled encouragingly at Scarlett. 'Shall we go in?' she said.

During that morning's lesson, Scarlett never really recovered from the surprise. She tried to focus her attention but kept coming back to what she saw as this latest betrayal by her one-time best friend. She really didn't understand what was going on with Gemma.

Miss Kitty tried to keep Scarlett focused on the lesson and gave her no chance to talk about what was on her mind, but eventually she could see this strategy wasn't working and told Scarlett to take a short break.

Immediately Scarlett brought up one of the things that was troubling her. Trying to sound casual, she said, 'I didn't realise Gemma was starting lessons with you.'

'This was her first one today,' said Miss Kitty.

'She never told *me*,' Scarlett said, not so casually.

'Well, now, that's up to Gemma, my dear.'

'But it's not fair!' she finally blurted out. 'I found you first.'

'And I didn't even know I was lost,' Miss Kitty teased her. 'You aren't my only pupil, Scarlett,' she said more seriously.

Scarlett breathed deeply. She knew that and began to feel very silly.

'I didn't get the part I wanted, either,' she said miserably.

'Ah,' said Kitty. 'So that's it. And what did you get?'

'Iago.' Scarlett saw Miss Kitty look up briefly to the ceiling and smile. 'It was Gemma's fault. I think she hates me.'

'Now, that would seem awfully unlikely, Scarlett. Aren't you the best of friends?' Kitty reminded her.

'We *were*,' Scarlett said, feeling stupidly tearful. She was trying so hard to be sensible but she could feel herself losing it.

Miss Kitty put an arm around Scarlett's shoulder. 'Let's talk about Iago. This is a fine result, in my opinion. It'll be a great challenge.'

Scarlett's heart sank at the sound of that word again. The way she was feeling she wasn't sure she wanted any more *challenges*.

Miss Kitty continued, 'Villains, and I mean *real* villains, are an absolute gift for an actor. Ah, doesn't

98

the audience always love a villain? And would you like to know why?' Scarlett nodded despite herself. 'Because it's the villain that carries the *energy*, which is the very lifeblood of the play.' Here, at least, was something Miss Kitty and Mr Coe seemed to agree on.

'That kind of energy...why, it's seductive... compelling...*irresistible*,' Kitty said with relish. 'All the great villains have it: Richard III, Lady Macbeth, Dracula, Fagin, Iago. Villains, my dear, have all the best lines and that's a fact.'

Scarlett couldn't help but be impressed by Miss Kitty's little speech. It certainly cast a different light on the matter. Immediately a whole rogue's gallery popped into Scarlett's mind: Cruella de Ville, Captain Hook, Darth Vader, Count Olaf...

As soon as she got home she would write a list in her journal: *Villainous Parts to Die For*.

There and then, Scarlett decided to make villains her speciality, and the nastier the better. She curled her lip and bared her teeth, already practising *glowering and grimacing*, but Miss Kitty, who always had a way of bringing her back to earth with a bump, soon put a stop to that.

'Enough with the faces, child, now back to the lesson.'

Later that day, in the privacy of her bedroom, Scarlett stared at herself one-eyed in the mirror. Improvising a patch, she crayoned a moustache on her face and experimented with blacking out one or two of her teeth with felt pen. It made her look spectacularly evil, if she said so herself.

She heaped one insult after another on her own reflection: 'You scurvy wretch! You miserable snivelling wastrel! You pathetic excuse for a pirate...'

Already Scarlett could see the attractions of villainy. She made a mental note to ask for a sword for her next birthday. Sword-fighting would be an invaluable skill. In the meantime she grabbed a ruler off her desk and made a few lunges at herself in the mirror. But as hard as Scarlett kept on trying to distract herself, her mind eventually came back to the puzzling question of Gemma.

When she'd got home, Scarlett had told her mum about Gemma starting lessons with Miss Kitty, expecting her mum to be as surprised as she was. But she had only said, 'Oh, that's good, isn't it? I gave

Gemma's mum Miss Kitty's number when she rang yesterday.'

'You *knew*?' Scarlett asked, amazed. She couldn't believe her own mother had known about this *piece of betrayal*.

'Yes. Is it a problem?'

'No-o-o,' said Scarlett. '*I suppose not*. But why didn't she tell me? What's with the big secret?'

'Perhaps she thought you might not be pleased,' her mum shrugged.

'Why wouldn't I be pleased?' Scarlett snapped.

Her mum did the thing that Scarlett often did herself: lifted one eyebrow higher than the other, without saying anything.

'I *am* pleased,' Scarlett insisted. 'I just wish she'd told me.'

'Well, Gemma must have had her reasons,' Mum said, closing the conversation.

Scarlett would have liked to ring Gemma and ask her what those reasons were, but she didn't feel she could. All week Scarlett had tried to carry on as if nothing was wrong, but she had known something was going on with Gemma.

When Scarlett had told Gemma about her dad's

six-week trip across the Atlantic and how much she was going to miss him, Gemma had only muttered, 'It's all right for some...' which wasn't the response Scarlett had been looking for.

Since her dad had set off on his trip they had only heard from him twice – the first time when he'd briefly docked in Madeira, and then again when he'd arrived in the Canary Islands. But Scarlett knew that soon, when he really headed out to sea, there would be no stops and only very occasional calls from the boat itself. Scarlett would have given anything, even the precious play, to be with her dad on his trip.

Now Scarlett wasn't only missing her dad, she was missing her best friend, too. It was making her feel quite *scratchy*. She pestered her mum to watch a DVD with her – or to take her shopping, or to go for a walk, anything in fact, but her mum had work to catch up with before Monday, as well as a pile of housework.

Jenny was a speech and language therapist, and like her husband, she often brought work home, which was hard for Scarlett, especially at times like this. In the end her mum had become quite irritable with her.

'For goodness' sake, Scarlett, you could tidy your

bedroom, or go for a bike ride, or watch TV, or ring Gemma. Or some other friends.'

But Scarlett hadn't really got other friends, at least no one she could just pick up the phone and call out of the blue on a Sunday afternoon.

Cleo had often told her it was a bad strategy relying on one person. Cleo herself preferred having lots of friends. She was closeted in her bedroom with two of them now: Jude and Jodie – Cleo-clones, as Scarlett thought of them. They were probably planning some new campaign to save the whale or the world.

Scarlett mooched around a bit longer until Jenny finally suggested she could help her clean some windows in the lounge – and suddenly Scarlett remembered some pressing thing she had to do in her bedroom.

Scarlett turned once more to her journal for distraction. It always offered some entertaining reading. In fact she frequently found herself laughing out loud. She looked back now through her past successes.

Julius Caesar had probably been Scarlett's biggest role and marked the beginning of her fascination with dying dramatically. Her second favourite part was when she played Napoleon in *Animal Farm*. Now *there* was a villain. She'd forgotten how much she'd enjoyed being the Big Bad Pig, yelling at Abbie and Brogan, who were playing a pair of sheep who couldn't learn to read: 'It's a *B*, you stupid animals...a *B*!!! *You're as stupid as the chickens!*'

But Scarlett hadn't only enjoyed the times when she'd played leading parts. Once the class had worked with a student teacher on a Spike Milligan poem called 'The Ning Nang Nong', and she, Gemma and Abbie had been chosen to play three teapots with only a couple of lines in the chorus! Scarlett had been disgusted at first. The other two girls were content to skive during the lessons, but Scarlett had come up with the idea of playing their parts completely over the top – like diva teapots. She'd played hers in the style of Madonna, and Mr Coe, watching from the doorway, admitted that he had never seen anything quite like it before! Nor had the student teacher. In the end she had redesigned the whole piece, giving the teapots the starring role.

It was the first time that Scarlett had really understood what Mr Coe had meant about there being no small parts, only small actors.

Looking through her past triumphs had given Scarlett a sudden surge of energy. She just *had* to get up and put on her music and dance, for a few minutes completely forgetting all her worries. In fact, she was so engrossed she didn't notice her sister standing in the bedroom doorway watching her.

'You seem to have cheered up,' Cleo observed, but Scarlett was so much in the groove she didn't even respond. She didn't see her sister shaking her head and wondering what far-flung planet Scarlett had come from.

Scarlett, as so often, was on her very own planet and it felt like a pretty great place to be.

Chapter Eight

Art mirrors life...

Whenever they were working on a new production, before they had even started on the script, Mr Coe liked to explore the emotional side of the play. So, the following Tuesday at Drama Club, he set the girls a new improvisation exercise.

He asked them to get into groups of three, and within each group label themselves A, B and C. To Scarlett's surprise, Gemma turned away, as if looking for another pair to which she could attach herself. But most of the other girls were already in threes and she reluctantly turned back to Scarlett. There was an awkward moment where the two girls stood waiting to see who would be left. To make matters worse Mr Coe directed Eve to join them as their C.

The teacher sent the Cs off into a corner while he talked to the As and Bs, asking them to imagine a short scene in which they excluded C, without explaining why. He urged them to be subtle about it, not even admitting that's what they were doing. Later they would all swap round. He wanted them to notice how it felt to be on different sides of the group.

No one liked the sound of this exercise; Scarlett and Gemma looked particularly uncomfortable. They had so far avoided discussing Gemma's lessons with Miss Kitty because Scarlett was behaving as if it had been her idea in the first place. But they felt just as awkward about having to work with Eve.

Since Mr Coe had drawn attention to the fact, all the girls realised that they still referred to Eve as *the new girl*, even though she'd been at the school for over six months. No one had made much effort to get to know her and everyone felt guilty about this – Scarlett and Gemma included.

As Eve walked towards them, Gemma groaned, 'I don't want to do this stupid thing.'

Nor did Scarlett, but she tried to remind herself that it was only a drama exercise after all. She at least could be professional. She quickly threw herself into the role.

'I don't like *her*, do you?' she asked Gemma, clearly

overacting. 'I think she's stuck up, coming to our school, getting the best part in the play, thinking she's something special. I think we should give her the freeze treatment.'

To Scarlett's horror, Gemma looked at her as if she meant it. The look clearly said: *I know you're really jealous that Eve got the part and you didn't. You're just pretending you're pretending.*

Scarlett was tempted to tell Gemma, 'It's called acting, you doughnut.'

Eve didn't seem any more prepared to play her part than Gemma, and even though Scarlett acted her socks off the two girls gave her nothing back. Things didn't improve when Gemma swapped roles with Eve, but when it was Scarlett's turn to play the outsider she was amazed by how seriously Gemma suddenly started to take the exercise.

'Hi there,' Scarlett said pleasantly, racing over to them as if they were both her long-lost friends. Gemma looked her up and down, as if Scarlett had crawled from beneath a rotting piece of wood, and then turned her back on her. Eve, a little embarrassed at first, soon began to follow Gemma's lead.

'So what's up?' Scarlett asked brightly.

Eve shrugged. 'Nothing.'

'Well, something's going on,' Scarlett said, helping them as much as she could. 'Have I got smelly breath or something?'

'I don't know what on earth you mean,' Gemma said coldly.

'Neither do I,' Eve agreed, and the girls physically moved a little closer together.

Scarlett began to feel like a genuine outcast. Every time she tried to penetrate the brick wall the two girls were putting up, she failed. Then Eve and Gemma started a conversation that deliberately excluded Scarlett, completely freezing her out. It was as if she didn't even exist.

Scarlett tried to stay in role, playing this Tigger-like character who just kept coming back for more, but she began to think that even Tigger – given this kind of treatment – would finally lose his bounce.

Scarlett was heartily relieved when the whole exercise was over and not surprised to find that all the other groups had struggled too. Mr Coe smiled knowingly.

'It's important for you to start to understand what Othello might have experienced as an outsider in this community,' he told them. 'I wanted you to see how many small and subtle ways we have to make people feel they're not welcome; they don't really belong. I wanted you all to be more aware of what it feels like to be on the receiving end of that.'

After the awkwardness of the exercise everyone was glad to finally turn to the play itself. Mr Coe asked them to begin by retelling the story of the play, which he'd told them the week before.

Scarlett, as usual, volunteered to start them off. 'It's about this general in the Venice army. He's the top guy...the hero of the play,' she added, with a tinge of disappointment.

'It starts with him sneaking off in the night to marry Desdemona, which is a bit out of order,' Brogan carried on.

'Yeah, but you can't blame him: he's black and she's white,' Leah pointed out. 'Nobody's gonna like that.'

'He's not definitely black,' Abbie reminded them.

'Whatever!' said Leah.

'Let's just carry on,' Mr Coe said encouragingly.

'There's this evil dude called Yago or something,' said Brogan.

'*I-ago*,' Scarlett corrected her. If she had to play

the wretched part she at least wanted people to get the name right.

'Why does everyone keep calling him *honest* Iago,' Zara wanted to know, 'when he's really a lying, cheating creep?'

'Yeah,' Leah agreed. 'How come no one sees that?'

'Good question,' Mr Coe agreed.

'He worms his way in so people start to trust him,' said Abbie.

'But how does he do that?' Mr Coe pressed them.

'By being cleverer than everyone else,' said Scarlett.

She saw Gemma look at her as if to say: *you would say that now it's your part.*

'Where does Bianca come in?' Mr Coe asked.

'That's to do with the handkerchief,' Brogan explained. 'The one Othello gave Desdemona as a present and she drops on the floor.'

'Oh, Mr Coe, I've got one we can use in the play,' Scarlett offered, enthusiastically. 'It's a fancy lace one of my grandma's. Shall I bring it in?'

'Thank you, Scarlett. What happens next?'

'Iago nicks it,' Leah continued.

'*Emilia* nicks it,' Abbie corrected her. 'Then she gives it to Iago.'

'And he plants it in Cassio's house,' said Minnie.

'Right. This is where Bianca comes in,' Mr Coe said. 'She's Cassio's girlfriend...'

The girls rolled their eyes. They all knew what that really meant.

'He finds the handkerchief and gives it to Bianca, not realising where it's come from,' he continued.

'Ah,' said Brogan, the light dawning, 'so Othello thinks Desdemona gave it to Cassio because they're having an affair.'

'Good,' said Mr Coe. 'Now where does Roderigo come in? Gemma?'

Gemma looked a bit vacant, as if she'd been thinking of other things. 'He's a rich guy who's been trying to get Desdemona to marry him, and he's gutted when she marries Othello instead.'

'Iago tells Roderigo she's having an affair with Cassio to make him even more jealous, to get him on his side in his plot against Othello,' Scarlett carried on.

'I don't buy it,' Brogan interrupted. 'Why would she have an affair when she's already got the top guy?'

'Cassio's younger, he's handsome, he's sexy. *He's the man!*' Leah said, rolling her eyes and wiggling her hips, making the other girls laugh.

Mr Coe told them they'd made an excellent start. Then he went on to encourage the girls to maintain their roles around school. For example, he told them, they should start to treat Eve as they would Othello: be deferential towards her, making way for her to pass, offering her their seat – and the same towards Desdemona.

'Yeah, too right, you peasants,' Brogan told the other girls. 'Down on your knees when you see me.'

But when Mr Coe went on to say that he wanted Brogan and Eve to try to get close and behave like a newly married couple, Brogan soon stopped smiling.

'Aw, Mr Coe, I don't want this smelly part. Can't I swap with Zara?'

Zara looked as if she'd have jumped at the chance, but Mr Coe quickly squashed any early signs of rebellion. 'No, Brogan, the casting is final. You will get into the part, I promise you.'

'But she's such a...*girl*,' she groaned.

'She may be a girl, but she's a strong, complex character. She's actually quite a feminist in the way she stands up for herself and insists on going off to war with Othello, rather than be left behind like the other women. She's quite feisty. A bit like you really.'

Brogan wasn't convinced, but Mr Coe was clearly not to be moved on this.

He then encouraged Scarlett and Gemma to work on their relationship, copying the way Roderigo follows Iago round like a puppy, doing everything he tells him.

Scarlett nodded enthusiastically. She was as eager as ever to take on Mr Coe's ideas; she didn't notice Gemma's lack of enthusiasm. This wasn't a million miles away from their actual relationship, Gemma thought, and a bit too much like art mirroring life for her liking.

When Drama Club was over, Scarlett was keen to make a start on Mr Coe's suggestions and invited Gemma back to her house for tea. But Gemma refused, offering no explanation. Scarlett watched her disappear down the corridor and out of the building, as if she couldn't get away fast enough.

Scarlett was disappointed, but still mystified. It couldn't be anything *she'd* done, or obviously she'd know about it. It must definitely be hormones. Fortunately Scarlett was well used to Cleo and *her* moods. Thank goodness, Scarlett thought, that at least *she* was an easy-going and even-tempered sort of person, and an all-round cool kind of character.

When Scarlett got home, however, and found she'd missed a rare call from her dad, she wasn't at all cool about it.

'It's not fair!' she wailed, throwing her bag across the lounge carpet. 'He *knows* Tuesday and Thursday are Drama Club nights.'

'You can't expect Dad to remember your daily timetable. He's got a lot on his mind,' Cleo reminded her.

'Like what?' Scarlett demanded. 'He's only on a boat in the middle of the Atlantic.'

'They're having quite a lot of problems with it,' Mum explained. 'It's hard to make calls from the yacht because it seems the communication system's faulty. He can only ring when they dock.'

'I thought this was a new boat! What's going to happen once they really head out to sea?' Scarlett asked. 'We won't hear from him for weeks then. How will we know if the boat capsizes and Dad gets eaten by sharks!'

Her mum wearily shook her head. 'It'll probably get fixed soon.'

'It'd better,' Scarlett warned no one in particular.

'How did the first rehearsal go?' Mum asked, changing the subject.

'All right,' Scarlett replied, grudgingly.

'Just all right?'

'Yes.' Scarlett sighed and threw herself down on the sofa. 'What's for tea?'

'What do you feel like?' Mum asked.

Scarlett felt like mashed bananas on toast with a spoonful of sugar on top. This was her idea of comfort food, something she'd been given when she was little and feeling ill and sorry for herself. Invalid food, Mum called it. She somehow knew her mum wouldn't think it a suitable meal for supper.

'Anything, as long as it's not got *beans* in it,' she growled, then knowing it would wind her mum up even more, added, 'I don't want any fart-food.'

Jenny was far too tired to pick Scarlett up on her language right now. She just rolled her eyes and ignored it.

Scarlett knew she was pushing her luck but she couldn't help herself. When she thought about how long it would be before she saw her dad again, her eyes filled with tears. At least she had the good sense not to cry in front of her mum and upset her too. Scarlett rushed to her bedroom to pull herself together.

She lay on her bed and gave herself a very firm talking-to. She reminded herself that her namesake, Scarlett O'Hara, was never seen crying. Even when civil war was raging around her, and both her parents were dying, and her beloved home, Tara, was burning down round her ears, Scarlett O'Hara came out fighting instead.

Scarlett sat up, blew her nose very hard and made herself get up to do some mirror work and maybe start learning her lines. Scarlett O'Hara's was a hard act to follow, but she was determined to try.

Chapter Nine

More sinn'd against than sinning.

As the week went on, Scarlett relied more and more on that Scarlett O'Hara energy. Without it, she would have been even more disturbed by the way that Gemma was now behaving. It was particularly puzzling to her because she and Gemma still hadn't had a proper argument. She had tried a few times to find out why Gemma was avoiding her, but Gemma flatly refused to talk about it. Each time she dismissed Scarlett with the same line. It began to have a very familiar ring to it: *I don't know what you mean.*

What further surprised Scarlett was seeing Gemma getting pally with Eve. Once or twice she had come across them talking together and tried to join in, only to find herself feeling as if she were back in that dreaded drama exercise.

'OK, very funny,' she'd said the first time, thinking it

was their idea of a joke. But when they just gave her blank looks Scarlett asked what was going on.

'*I don't know what you mean,*' Gemma shrugged.

Then both girls went silent, as if they were waiting for Scarlett to leave so that they could carry on their private conversation – probably about her!

Oh, please yourselves, she thought, suddenly weary of the whole business. Everyone but her seemed to be going slowly off their rockers.

This opinion was only confirmed when, a couple of days later in the cafeteria, Scarlett plonked herself down as usual in the midst of the other girls, dramatically opening her lunchbox to start the bidding in the lunchtime trading.

'What am I bid! What am I bid!' she barked, holding up a Tracker in one hand and a banana in the other.

Every day the girls traded their lunches and Scarlett often presided over it. There was a recognised value system with chocolate bars like Yorkies and Trackers at the top, representing the hottest trades, followed by Hula Hoops, Pringles and tuna wraps all the way down to raisins, bananas and carrots. These last, far-too-healthy options, were almost impossible to shift.

Today, despite the fact that Scarlett was holding up a Tracker – a very hot item – no one was showing any interest at all. In fact the girls went on eating their own lunches as if Scarlett wasn't even there.

After fooling about with her banana, which seemed to amuse no one, Scarlett gave up and settled down to eat. She felt awkward, as if she'd blundered into some private conversation between the other girls.

'So, what's up?' she asked.

The other girls shrugged, shook their heads and looked down at their lunchboxes. Scarlett laughed. This was getting past a joke.

'Come on,' she said. 'I haven't grown an extra head or anything.'

In the end Zara broke the silence. 'We're only doing what Mr Coe said.'

'What do you mean?' Scarlett asked, still no wiser.

'You're the *villain*, aren't you?' Zara spelt it out.

And then, as one, the girls closed their boxes, got up from the table and walked away, leaving Scarlett sitting alone, upset and confused.

It was only after they'd all disappeared that Scarlett thought, *that's not right!* It isn't until the end of the play that everyone realises Iago is the villain. Until then everyone think he's a great guy; they call him honest Iago, everybody's friend. Trust those doughnuts to get it wrong, she told herself.

She shook her head, then tucked into her food. It would take more than that kind of nonsense to put Scarlett off her lunch.

By the end of the day, however, Scarlett was beginning to feel as if she seriously *had* grown a second head. She'd given up asking what was going on, because the girls insisted they didn't know what she was talking about. She was starting to feel as if she were going mad and imagining it all. She was wondering how she could get to the bottom of it, when the answer came unexpectedly.

They had just finished PE, the last lesson of the day. It had been a boring affair for Scarlett, who'd been given the chill treatment the whole lesson. When they got back to the changing rooms she was on the point of confronting the person she saw as the likely ringleader – Zara.

Scarlett had her back to the other girls, taking much longer folding her clothes than she would normally have done. She was still planning what she might say when she noticed how quiet everyone else had gone behind her. Scarlett turned to see all the girls lined up in a row facing her. She swallowed hard. For one awful moment she imagined they were about to beat her up.

So she was a little relieved when one by one the girls went into a little mime routine. First Zara licked her lips, pressing them together in an exaggerated fashion and widening her eyes like Bambi. Abbie shook her head and neighed; Brogan squared her shoulders and huffed and puffed like an engine. Even though they had never actually *seen* Scarlett imitate them, each girl did a fair imitation of Scarlett imitating her – all except Gemma, who stood with them looking very uncomfortable but also saying nothing.

At first, Scarlett couldn't believe what she was seeing. Nor could she believe that Gemma would have given her away like this. It felt like the final betrayal.

Scarlett knew she had no argument to offer, not a leg to stand on, but she still felt compelled to try. 'Look, guys, I never meant anything…'

But it was too late; the girls did another disappearing act and Scarlett was left alone in the cloakroom, in no doubt now that Gemma had finally broken their friendship. She'd also made sure that none of the other girls would want to be friends with Scarlett either. She picked up her neatly folded clothes and stuffed them roughly into her bag.

'*Oh, rats,*' she moaned to herself. It had only ever been a bit of fun. But then Scarlett quickly corrected herself: actually it had been a bit of serious acting practice. If anyone was to blame here it was Mr Coe. He was the one who'd encouraged them to *study* other people. And now look where it had got her.

On her way home, Scarlett asked herself some difficult questions: did she really deserve to be the least popular girl in the world? Was she really a horrible person? Scarlett didn't think so. She knew she wasn't perfect, that she had her faults like everyone else. Cleo reminded her of those on a daily basis.

For instance, Scarlett knew she had a stubborn streak; she couldn't bear to back down. Not that she believed this was always a bad thing. It meant that when she took something on – like an acting role – she didn't easily give up. On the other hand, it meant that if anyone dared her to do something – even something pretty silly – she usually found it impossible to say no.

But Scarlett wasn't the kind of person to wriggle out of unpleasant things either. She hadn't tried to deny she'd been imitating her friends. Still, she couldn't imagine if one of them had imitated her she'd lose much sleep over it. *She'd* have treated it as a joke. But then Scarlett prided herself on having a sense of humour, something her friends seemed to have collectively mislaid. And it was a pretty mean act on Gemma's part to tell them in the first place.

By the time she got home, Scarlett had pretty well persuaded herself that, in the words of the mighty bard, she was *more sinned against than sinning*.

At the end of this appalling day the only thing that could cheer Scarlett up was getting to speak to her dad. When Steve rang after supper, Scarlett had never felt happier to hear his voice. He was ringing from Cap Verde.

'Where's that?' she asked.

'Look at the map, why don't you?' Cleo told her. She'd marked their dad's route on it in red ink and stuck it on the kitchen wall.

'It's off the African coast, south of the Canaries,' her dad said. 'From here we head west towards the Caribbean. There'll be no stopping from now until we get there. I don't want you worrying about me if you don't hear for a week or so. If the communications fail again I may not be able to call. But I will, if I possibly can. You take care of each other. I love you all.'

'Love you, Dad,' Scarlett said.

'Love you lots,' Cleo said on the other phone.

'Love you more,' Scarlett said.

The girls hung up while Mum had a last word with Dad.

'Why do you always do that?' Cleo asked, irritably.

'Do what?'

'Always have to go one better.'

But Scarlett had had enough of people with no sense of humour. 'Oh, get a life,' she snapped. She made a dramatic exit, slamming the doors on her way, and retired to the peace of her bedroom.

Although Scarlett was glad to have talked to her dad, it only reminded her how much she was missing him. She lay on her bed feeling sorry for herself. But when Mum came up to see she was all right, Scarlett shrugged it off.

Scarlett didn't tell her mum what had happened at school, partly because she felt embarrassed. She might have told Dad, if he'd been there, because he would

126

probably have seen the funny side of it. She wasn't sure her mum would.

So Scarlett stayed on her bed, half-heartedly learning her lines, with her music on so loud she didn't hear the knock on her bedroom door. She was surprised when Uncle Gerry's head suddenly appeared round it.

'Why are you hiding in your bedroom like a bear with a sore paw?'

Scarlett very nearly poured out the whole story. But she decided against it, pretending she was just struggling to learn her lines. Gerry offered to help. Scarlett hesitated – this was always her dad's job – but in the end she was glad to have the company and handed the script over.

Gerry sat on the floor leaning against her bed, while Scarlett paced the room, reciting her lines, and doing appropriate gestures to better feel the part. It was hard for her to keep her concentration, though, when she turned to see Gerry wearing her Lion King pyjama case on his head.

'What?' he asked completely seriously as Scarlett burst out laughing.

It was the same silly kind of joke her father would

have pulled, and Scarlett immediately thought of him again.

'I bet you're missing your dad,' Gerry said, as if reading her thoughts.

Scarlett nodded.

'He was like you: good at learning things,' Gerry said. 'He always did his homework. Not like me.'

'Have you and Dad always been friends?' Scarlett asked.

'Since we were eight. Some older kids were beating me up and your dad waded in and sent them flying. He was always a big fellow.'

Scarlett smiled. She loved that about her dad. 'What else was he like?'

'A bit of a geek, really, but that never stopped him getting the girls. I could never work it out. I used to tell him he was *born lucky*.'

Scarlett had seen photographs of her mum and dad when they were young, and there were a couple of videos, but she would have loved to have actually known them as children. She thought it wasn't fair that your mum and dad would know you when you were a kid *and* when you were a grown-up; you only knew them as adults.

Later, when Scarlett went to the bathroom, she came back to find Gerry fast asleep on her bedroom carpet. He must have slid slowly to the side without waking himself up. The pyjama case was still half on his head.

He looked so funny that Scarlett raced downstairs and dragged her mum back upstairs to see. They stood in the bedroom doorway, Mum shaking her head and smiling. 'He must be really overworked with Dad away,' she whispered. 'He should go home, but I don't think he wants to.'

Scarlett frowned. As they stood watching him, he suddenly twitched and woke himself up. He looked like he must still be dreaming because he opened and closed his eyes, as if he was trying to make sense of where he was.

'You should get off home,' Mum said quietly.

In no time Gerry had recovered himself and was laughing it off.

'I thought I'd died and gone to hell,' he said, 'then I opened my eyes and saw you two looking like a pair of angels, so I knew it must be heaven.'

Scarlett stood at the front door with her mum waving Gerry off.

'Why doesn't he want to go home?' she asked Mum.

'I think he's got a lot of worries.'

'What kind of worries?'

But her mum did that infuriating thing she often did – answering a question with another question. 'Have you seen the time, young lady?'

Scarlett reluctantly got ready for bed. Before she went to sleep, she crossed another day off the calendar she had made. Her dad had been at sea for two weeks and four days, which left three weeks and three days still to go. It had seemed like forever already and he wasn't even halfway yet. *Twenty-four whole days left*, she thought.

Scarlett seriously doubted whether she would last that long. She wondered whether a person could actually die of missing someone. She decided that would be a long and lingering death and probably a rather boring affair. Scarlett dismissed it as having no dramatic impact. Not like a good stabbing, she thought!

Chapter Ten

It's called acting...

It wasn't a completely new experience for Scarlett to have to sit through what she called a *shambolic* rehearsal, listening to the other girls complaining about the parts they'd been given, and none of them knowing their lines. But in the past she would at least have had Gemma's company, and Gemma's sympathetic ear.

Today things had been even worse than usual. Brogan in particular was still rebelling against playing such a *girly* role. And Zara, who was feeling underused, spent her time distracting the other girls and making them giggle.

'For goodness' sake,' Mr Coe bawled, raking through his hair. 'Can you girls please pay attention and be ready for your cues. I wish you'd take a lead from Scarlett. She, at least, isn't wasting her energy gossiping.'

The other girls glared at Scarlett as she tried not to look like a goody-goody. The truth was, Scarlett privately agreed with them; she didn't want the role she'd been given either. And she wasn't sitting alone in order to stay focused, but because no one else would sit with her.

Scarlett was painfully aware now of what it felt like to be the outsider. She realised how Eve must have been feeling all this time, although being ignored wasn't quite the same as being scowled at and talked about by everyone else.

Unkind comments kept drifting over her way. When Leah had remarked what a crazy idea it was of Mr Coe's to make them all play against type, Zara had said that there was *one person* who wasn't playing against type and they all knew who that was! All heads had swivelled and looked in Scarlett's direction.

But if Scarlett had been anything like Iago surely she wouldn't be having so much trouble playing him, she reasoned. And she *was* having trouble, as she had recently confided in her journal.

Mr Coe says I have to find the Iago inside, but what if I can't? What if he's not

132

there? Mr Coe says he's driven by envy.
But I don't think I REALLY know what that
feels like.

Well, maybe that time Zara got those grey
suede boots...or when Leah went to Disney World
for half term...but that's not the same,
surely. I didn't want to DESTROY them, for
goodness' sake!

There must be something Shakespeare isn't
telling us!!!!!!!

It wasn't making things any easier for Scarlett that, as usual, she was getting conflicting advice from her two teachers. While Mr Coe continued to encourage identification with her character, Miss Kitty dismissed the whole Method approach as wrong-headed.

'If you'll forgive a bit of old-fashioned plain speaking, Scarlett, it's a load of horse manure. You don't have to *be* evil to *play* evil! That's the whole nonsense of Method acting in a nutshell.'

Miss Kitty told Scarlett that trying to work out why Iago is such a bad lot was a complete waste of time.

She reminded her that at the end of the play Shakespeare cleverly leaves Iago silent about why he's done it all.

'By refusing to explain himself Iago holds on to some of his power,' Miss Kitty explained. 'You can go on psychoanalysing him until the cows come home for milking, my dear, but you'll probably never discover his real motives. Iago is just a representation of evil and evil itself is often beyond explanation.'

Scarlett sighed heavily. While this gave her a lot more to think about, it still didn't actually tell her *how* to play the role.

'The audience want to hate Iago,' Miss Kitty went on, 'but they're drawn to him despite themselves. Villains are often very attractive people because of the energy they give off. Concentrate on the energy,' she advised. 'And just act!'

'When Laurence Olivier was making the film *Marathon Man* he told his young co-star Dustin Hoffman – who had stayed awake for two days so that he would look properly exhausted for a scene – *"You should try acting, my boy. It's much easier."*

'That's my advice to you, for what it's worth,'

Miss Kitty smiled. 'Just try acting, dear girl. It's what real actors do.'

Later that day Scarlett sat at home with a pile of DVDs in front of her. She'd spent the whole afternoon fast-forwarding to find some good examples of villains: Jack Sparrow in *Pirates of the Caribbean*, Captain Hook in the film *Hook*, Darth Vader in *Star Wars*. But the thing about most of them, Scarlett realised, was that they were self-confessed baddies: pantomime villains encouraging the audience to boo at them. Iago wasn't like any of them – he was much more devious.

She suddenly let out all her frustration in an ear-splitting yell: 'I DON'T UNDERSTAND THIS PART!'

Her mum and Cleo came running from different parts of the house.

'For goodness' sake, Scarlett, what's happened?' her mum demanded. 'I thought you'd really killed yourself this time.'

'I can't get into this part,' Scarlett whined. 'It's too hard.' She was lying on the carpet on her back, her arms and legs in the air, looking like a dead gerbil.

'Is that all?' said her mum, relieved.

'Oh, stop it,' Cleo told her. 'We've heard nothing but you moaning about this play for the last three weeks. You're boring the life out of us.'

'But it's driving me mad,' Scarlett moaned.

'*You're* driving *us* mad,' said Cleo irritably.

Their mum agreed. 'You really are trying my patience, Scarlett. I'm sure you wouldn't be behaving like this if Dad were at home.'

If Dad were at home, he'd have shown a bit more sympathy, Scarlett thought. He'd have told Scarlett what to do; he'd have sorted it all out for her.

Her dad would have had time for her. Nobody at school had, nor anyone at home, it seemed. She was feeling quite lonely and truly sorry for herself.

But luckily Scarlett soon tired of self-pity. She picked up a second DVD of *Othello* she'd found on Amazon and started to watch it. She'd only just got past the credits when the doorbell rang.

Scarlett raced to the door in the hope that whoever it was might provide some company. She was delighted to see Uncle Gerry and begged him to come and watch the film with her.

This one was an even older black-and-white version

in which Othello was played by an actor called Orson Welles. It was nicely creepy and had the feel of an old horror film.

Once or twice Scarlett turned to see Gerry's reaction, but he'd actually fallen asleep. This left her free to fast-forward the boring bits. When it was over, and Gerry had woken up, he pretended he'd seen more of it than he had.

'Mmm, he was a nasty piece of work,' he said of Iago.

'It still beats me why everyone trusts him,' Scarlett observed. 'He's so clearly up to no good – why can't anyone see that?'

'He's a good actor?' Gerry suggested. 'He takes everyone in.'

Scarlett dismissed this. 'He wouldn't have taken me in. I'd have seen through him.' Gerry smiled at her. 'Well, I would,' she insisted. 'You can always tell when someone's bad.'

'People are rarely *all* good or *all* bad,' Gerry told her.

But Scarlett didn't accept this either. People might be good and do bad things, but in that case they'd be sorry. If they weren't sorry, they were bad. It was as simple as that to Scarlett.

'Sometimes people find themselves in situations...' Gerry started to say.

'What kind of situations?' Scarlett asked.

Gerry sighed. 'Difficult situations...'

'Like what?' Scarlett persisted.

'I don't know...' He shook his head as if he'd completely lost his train of thought.

'Well, I'm sure I don't,' said Scarlett. 'What I do know is, *I'd* have smelled a rat and his name would have been Iago.'

'If only we all had your powers of deduction, Sherlock,' Gerry smiled.

Scarlett knew that Gerry was teasing her, but she thought he wasn't so far from the truth. Scarlett had conveniently forgotten how badly she'd misread her best friend. But she was still fully expecting Gemma to come to her senses – any day soon.

Gerry asked about the pile of DVDs on the carpet and Scarlett explained that she'd been searching for inspiration.

'You can help me decide,' she said, jumping up and giving Gerry a brief run through the different ways she might play Iago: as Captain Hook, Rumplestiltskin, Fagin, and finally Hannibal Lector.

She even copied the way he slavered his words: 'F-f-fava beans...'

'Mmm,' Gerry said, trying to stifle his laughter. 'I think Hannibal-Lector-meets-Iago would have everyone rolling in the aisles, but I suspect that isn't quite what Mr Coe has in mind.'

Scarlett sank back onto the sofa temporarily defeated.

Fortunately she had that vital stubborn streak that Miss Kitty told her all actors needed. Scarlett would never give up. Iago might get the better of the other characters in the play, but he would *not* get the better of Scarlett Lee. This time Iago had definitely met his match.

Chapter Eleven

When sorrows come...

Scarlett really didn't think things could get a whole lot worse: her dad had as good as disappeared off the planet, her best friend had totally abandoned her – just when she needed her most – and through an act of total betrayal had turned Scarlett into public enemy number one at school.

And, as if that wasn't enough, for the very first time Scarlett felt completely out of her depth in a play. There were only two weeks to go and, even to Scarlett, who was usually so optimistic, it all seemed daunting.

I think Mr Coe's advice to leave I CAN'T and I DON'T at the stage door is not as easy as it sounds – 'specially if you've got the hardest part in the whole play! 'Specially with everyone watching and waiting for you to fall splat on your face. They would just love that. They're all still giving me the big chill! But who cares! Scarlett Lee WILL NOT BE DEFEATED. This is a matter of HONOUR!

At school, to keep up her spirits, Scarlett had developed an odd but comforting little hum. She wanted to give the impression to the other girls that she was perfectly happy with her own company and didn't need theirs, thank you very much.

At home it was taking a little more effort. The hours between school finishing and going to bed were difficult to fill and Scarlett was sometimes so bored she felt like running around the house screaming.

Today, when the doorbell rang, Scarlett was delighted to find on the doorstep her old friends – as she now thought of them – DI Maddox and PC Dryer. There was also a female police officer called PC Brown, a bonus from Scarlett's point of a view.

'Hiya,' she said, beaming and inviting them all in.

'Is your mother at home?' DI Maddox asked, in a surprisingly formal manner.

'Mum!' Scarlett bawled upstairs, where her mum

was getting changed out of her work clothes. 'It's the police again.'

Scarlett's mother appeared on the landing and called down that she'd only be a minute. While they waited in the hallway DI Maddox smiled at Scarlett, but unlike last time, didn't try to engage her in conversation.

Cleo also appeared on the landing, apparently hesitating about whether to stay upstairs and keep her distance from PC Dryer, or come downstairs where she could keep Scarlett on a tighter rein. When Scarlett started grinning and dramatically rolling her eyes towards the young policeman, Cleo raced down. She was followed by their mum.

Scarlett fully expected them all to retire to the lounge or the kitchen for another cosy and entertaining interlude, so she was surprised and disappointed when DI Maddox held out a piece of paper and said to her mum, 'We have a warrant to search the house and to remove any documents belonging to your husband and pertaining to his business.'

Scarlett's mum laughed, which reassured Scarlett, who was also thinking it must be some kind of joke. But DI Maddox's face took on an even more serious expression as he asked to be shown to her father's study.

PC Dryer, who was looking more embarrassed than ever, kept his face studiously turned away from Cleo and seemed relieved when DI Maddox sent him off to remove their dad's computer.

'What's this all about?' Scarlett's mother asked, finally realising it was serious.

But DI Maddox said he wasn't in a position to give her any more information. The two young constables were already dismantling Dad's computer in his study, while DI Maddox looked around the other downstairs rooms. Mum followed him, asking over and over again what he was looking for.

Scarlett and Cleo tried to follow their mother but she closed the lounge door behind her in the hope that DI Maddox might be prepared to explain himself if the girls weren't present.

Scarlett felt bewildered. She had watched enough police dramas on TV to have seen this kind of thing happen but she would never in her wildest dreams have expected to see it enacted under her own roof. She was feeling slightly scared, but at the same time, if she were being completely honest, a little excited.

Mr Coe always impressed upon them that all life experience is like food and drink to an actor, valuable material they could call upon. Scarlett suddenly had an urge to run upstairs to get her notebook to make detailed notes, particularly about the female police officer, who had an interesting way of holding her head permanently at forty-five degrees, but Scarlett resisted the impulse in case she missed something and tried instead to commit it all to memory.

Usually, Scarlett didn't easily feel embarrassment – another emotion Cleo claimed she had been born without – but she was beginning to feel something rather like it now. She became aware of an inappropriate desire to laugh and before she could control herself, Cleo spotted it.

'You think this is funny?' she hissed at her sister.

Scarlett shook her head, trying to deny it.

'Wait till they start on your room, then we'll see who's laughing,' Cleo snapped.

This idea hadn't even occurred to Scarlett. Immediately she raced upstairs to tidy up, not because she was in the least bit house-proud, as her mum would have vouched, but because she did care about creating a serious impression.

She threw her discarded clothes into the linen basket and tidied her bed. Then she looked around, wondering what the policemen might be interested in – what possibly incriminating evidence might be lurking in her room. Her journal, of course – just the kind of thing they might seize. There was no way they were taking that.

Scarlett searched her brain for a place to hide it: under the mattress, in her wardrobe, in the linen basket – all far too obvious. In the end she slid it behind the radiator. (This proved to be a poor choice since it took her half an hour of poking with a ruler to get it out again later that evening!)

The main thing on Scarlett's desk was her computer. They'd already taken her dad's; she sincerely hoped they wouldn't take hers. It had all her school coursework on it, and her notes for *Othello*. Scarlett was determined they wouldn't take it and she raced downstairs to announce this.

But she found that her sister had beaten her to it. Cleo was standing in the hallway haranguing PC Dryer. 'I don't care what your orders are, you are not taking *my* computer! All my exam work's on it! I shall hold you personally responsible if I fail my exams. Take it from me and there will be consequences.'

Scarlett was secretly impressed with Cleo's speech. Once or twice PC Dryer had tried to interrupt Cleo's flow, but without success. It was only when she'd finished that he said with a smile, 'We won't be taking *anything* from your rooms, Miss.'

For a second the wind went out of Cleo's sails. 'That's just as well,' she snapped. 'And don't you *Miss* me,' she warned him, before storming upstairs.

Scarlett felt a moment's guilt when PC Dryer turned to her and they shared a smile at Cleo's expense.

Just then her mum and DI Maddox came out of the lounge, her mum looking very serious and a little upset. But when she saw Scarlett she smiled reassuringly.

'Sweetheart, would you go up to your room...'

'But, Mu-u-um...' Scarlett began. How could her mum seriously expect her to miss out on this exciting and invaluable experience?

'DI Maddox is just leaving and we'll talk about it when he's gone,' her mum said, physically directing Scarlett up the stairs.

As Scarlett reluctantly left what she liked to think of as the crime scene – although to her knowledge no crime had actually been committed – she overheard DI Maddox asking her mum, 'And you're quite sure you didn't know anything about this off-shore bank account?'

Despite the serious faces and hushed voices, Scarlett still couldn't take it all seriously, because deep down she knew there had to be a mistake. Even if there had been a crime it had nothing to do with her dad. She was absolutely sure of that.

As she passed Cleo's bedroom the door was open and Scarlett looked in.

'Have they gone yet?' Cleo asked crossly.

'Nearly. Mum's going to talk to us later. Do you think Dad will go to prison?' Scarlett asked, almost but not completely joking.

'Oh, for goodness' sake, Scarlett, don't be so ridiculous!' Cleo snapped. 'Why can't you just grow up?'

As she went off to her own room Scarlett further irritated her sister by muttering audibly: '*Scarlett*! Why can't you just *grow up*?'

Scarlett threw herself onto her bed and lay there,

running a little fantasy through her head in which her dad went to prison for life, and she and her mum and Cleo had to leave their nice comfy house and ended up living on the streets with all their belongings in a couple of black bin bags. It was such a moving and convincing picture that Scarlett found herself on the verge of tears.

Minutes later, when Cleo looked in on her, she was softened at the sight of her sister apparently crying.

'Come on,' she said, more gently than she sometimes did. 'I didn't mean to upset you.'

For once Scarlett had the good sense not to tell Cleo what had prompted the tears. Even she could see that her fantasy might have been a touch over-dramatic.

Later, when the family were gathered in the lounge, Jenny tried to reassure the girls that the whole thing must have a simple explanation. Something had clearly happened concerning Dad's business, and because he was *temporarily unavailable*, the police had said it was making it more difficult for them to eliminate him from their enquiries. They'd been reluctant, however, to tell Jenny exactly what it was they were enquiring into.

'Well, it can't be anything to do with Dad's number plates,' Cleo said. 'It seems a bit of a coincidence that they come about nothing in particular and the next thing they're back with a search warrant. I think he's being set up.'

'By whom?' Mum shook her head. 'I don't think we should jump to conclusions. If we could only reach Dad, I know he'd be able to clear it all up. Oh, thank goodness,' she said looking out of the window. 'It's Gerry. Perhaps he has some idea what's going on.'

Jenny went to the door and let Gerry in. Cleo and Scarlett could only make out odd words from the hall, until they heard their mum's voice rising, 'You *knew*?! And you didn't tell *me*! I can't believe it, Gerry!'

Scarlett and Cleo both jumped up and went out to the hall, but Gerry was already leading their mum in to sit down. He smiled at the girls.

'Listen, I didn't tell you because basically there's nothing to tell. It's just red tape, bureaucratic...VAT rubbish. I've given them all the information they need. They shouldn't be here troubling you. I've told them I can handle it.'

Jenny looked relieved for a moment and suddenly

started to cry. Scarlett went to sit with her mum and hold her hand. Gerry took out a handkerchief and gave it to her, then sat on the other side of Jenny, with a reassuring arm around her shoulders.

'I'm sorry, I'm probably being silly. I know there's nothing really to cry about,' she said apologetically.

'Listen,' Gerry told her, 'I promised Steve I'd look after you all and I meant it. First thing tomorrow I shall go down to the police station to complain. There's no grounds for them coming here doing a heavy number...even if there were...' he broke off. 'But I'm not even going to think about that possibility.'

'What possibility?' Cleo demanded.

'Nothing, Cleo,' Gerry told her. 'You know I'd trust your dad with my life.'

Scarlett watched her mum begin to calm down. She was so glad Gerry was here to help them. He would sort it all out. But Cleo didn't seem to share Scarlett's confidence. She turned on Gerry again, 'I think Mum's right. You should have said something. Why didn't you?'

'I told you why: I didn't want your mum wasting energy worrying about something that's absolutely not a problem. I was just trying to save you all from being upset. I'm sorry, Cleo, if you feel I've let you down.'

'Of course not,' Mum said, patting Gerry's hand. 'Cleo doesn't mean that. She's just a bit upset, aren't you, sweetheart?'

But Cleo refused to answer and angrily left the room. Gerry and their mum shrugged and for a second time that evening Scarlett found herself sharing a smile at her sister's expense.

Later when Scarlett went upstairs to get ready for bed, she found Cleo sulking in her room.

'There's no need to be so ratty with Gerry,' she told Cleo. 'It's not his fault. He's just trying to help.'

'So he says,' Cleo snapped. 'I'm sick of him hanging around here. You'd think he hadn't got a home of his own to go to.'

Scarlett was shocked. 'I thought you liked Gerry,' she said.

'He gets on my nerves,' Cleo replied. '*Why is he always here*?' she demanded, as if Scarlett had the answer.

'He's Dad's best friend,' Scarlett said.

'We'll see about that,' Cleo said cryptically.

Scarlett shook her head and left her sister to her

sulks. This was presumably to do with Cleo's growing dislike of men in general, Scarlett thought. But whatever the reasons, she was beginning to form the opinion that her sister might be finally losing the plot.

By the time Scarlett had finally retrieved her journal from behind the radiator and climbed into bed it was gone ten o'clock. But she was far too excited to sleep.

My life has taken a really exciting turn lately. I think at last I might be getting A STORY! It's not every day there's a police raid on your house. They even had a SEARCH WARRANT. What on earth can it all be about? I hope I find out soon.

It's a drag, though, having no one to share it all with. I wish Gemma would hurry up and get over herself.

Scarlett was beginning to find that life wasn't half as much fun without an audience.

Chapter Twelve

That men should put an enemy in their mouths...

As the week went on, things didn't improve for Scarlett. The rest of the girls were still giving her the freeze treatment. At Thursday's rehearsal, sitting on her own again, she ran another little fantasy through her head, imagining, if she really were a villain like Iago, what kinds of revenge she might wreak on the other girls.

For a start she would steal Zara's precious lip-gloss, then buy up all the local supplies and dispose of those too so she had to go cold turkey. She'd force Brogan into some horribly girly outfit – with bows in her hair – and tie Leah's hands behind her back so she couldn't do her incessant drumming – like she'd been doing for the last five minutes right behind Scarlett and driving her mad!

Scarlett tried to ignore Leah, even though she knew she was doing it on purpose. She was determined to keep up her convincing performance of someone fully occupied with her own amusing thoughts. But this only seemed to make the other girls more determined to keep on trying to wind her up.

When Mr Coe finally arrived the girls were expecting to rehearse the handkerchief scene. This was an important moment, he had told them, because the handkerchief was the only real piece of evidence of Desdemona's alleged affair. Such a very small thing, he stressed, to build a whole plot upon.

While they were waiting for the teacher the girls messed around with the handkerchief – Scarlett's handkerchief – each *pretending* to blow her nose on it. Scarlett *pretended* to be completely indifferent – as if the handkerchief were nothing to her, which only drove the girls to more extremes of silliness. When Mr Coe breezed in, he took one look at them and decided to postpone the handkerchief scene. The girls clearly needed settling down before any serious work could be done. He chose instead an exercise he often used, called Hot Seating.

Whoever was chosen had to sit in the middle of

the group – on the hot seat – and speak about her character for a minute or two, then try to answer questions the other girls fired at her.

Hot seating felt a bit like a party game, but it had the serious intention of making the girls think more deeply and more precisely about the kind of person they were playing. The questions might be light and seemingly frivolous, for example, *if your character was a piece of furniture, what might it be?* Or they could be more serious and searching: *when your character was a child, what was he/she most scared of?*

Scarlett usually adored this game, especially if she was the one on the hot seat, getting all the attention, but today she wasn't a bit happy to be chosen.

'Iago – tell us all about yourself.' Mr Coe started things off.

'I'm a villain,' Scarlett began, playing safe and stating the obvious. 'I'm clever...and devious...' Mr Coe nodded encouragingly. 'I'm envious of Othello, because he's got all the power *and* a beautiful wife.' She could see all the other girls looking bored and Mr Coe waiting for her to tell him something they hadn't already talked about a hundred times before.

And...seemed to hang in the air.

Scarlett took a deep breath. 'And I like tricking people; I get a buzz out of it. It's like a power trip.'

'Excellent!' Mr Coe told her. Scarlett beamed. She hadn't realised she knew that until she said it; Scarlett often did her best thinking aloud. 'The thing is,' she continued, 'I'm always behind other people – Othello – and then Cassio – and I hate it. I want to be the top banana, because I'm as clever as they are.'

Finally she had a tiny glimpse of something she could really recognise. Scarlett had been in situations like that: standing by and watching someone else do something she knew she could do better. She sometimes felt that way watching Eve play Othello.

But Scarlett wasn't left to feel pleased with herself for long. When Mr Coe invited the other girls to join in it was as if they had all prepared their questions – like weapons – in advance. Zara led the attack.

'Did you ever have any friends, when you were at school?' she asked innocently. 'And if so, did you ever poke fun at them behind their backs?'

Scarlett didn't know how to answer that question, which clearly had nothing to do with Iago and everything to do with her. But the girls were eager to get in their own little attack disguised as a question.

'If you were a snake,' Brogan hissed, 'what kind of snake would you be?'

'If you wanted to murder someone, what method would you use?' Abbie asked mildly. 'Stab them in the back?'

The questions were coming thick and fast and everyone hit the bullseye.

'OK,' Mr Coe cut in. 'Give Scarlett a chance to reply. Remember, the purpose of the exercise is to *help* her, not to catch her out.'

But Scarlett sat there uncharacteristically tongue-tied and no amount of time was going to help her. After all the others had attacked, she waited for the final cutting question from Gemma, but it never came. Scarlett wasn't sure what this said about Gemma's feelings, but she was left in no doubt about the message the other girls were sending her: she was still right out in the cold. Even Eve was far more accepted now as part of the group. Scarlett felt embarrassed and, as much as she hated to admit it, defeated.

Mr Coe was disappointed that the exercise seemed to have backfired. Scarlett looked less confident than before they'd started. He tried to sum up for the girls. 'Iago is a complex and fascinating study of evil. He seems to be without conscience – a clever and ruthless opportunist. And yet throughout the play he's liked, respected and *trusted* by everyone. How do you think he manages that?'

At last Gemma spoke up. 'He's acting – all the time.'

'Exactly,' said Mr Coe. 'He only *seems* to be a genuine and trustworthy person. This whole play is about Appearance and Reality. Iago pretends to be everyone's friend, but in truth he's only ever thinking of himself.'

Scarlett felt the other girls giving her sideways, knowing looks – especially Gemma. Why on earth did they keep on mixing her up with the character she was playing? *For goodness' sake*, she wanted to yell at them, *it's Iago he's talking about – not me – you doughnuts! Get a reality check!*

On her way home from Drama Club, Scarlett had to call in at Miss Kitty's to collect some forms for her next exam, which was coming up soon. She found Miss Kitty in the kitchen, listening to the radio while she unloaded the dishwasher. She offered Scarlett some juice and a piece of flapjack and Scarlett took off her coat and made herself at home.

Miss Kitty was in a reminiscing mood, which Scarlett always enjoyed. Today she was full of stories of her time in Africa with her missionary husband. 'It was where I got my first taste for acting,' she told Scarlett. 'I made up plays for the wee-uns in the villages and we acted them out. Sure, I stole most of the ideas from Shakespeare, but then if you're going to steal, steal from the master, I always say. And how is your play doing?' she asked Scarlett. 'Are we getting to grips with Iago?'

Scarlett shrugged and tried to raise a smile. 'OK, I guess.'

Miss Kitty could see this was not the case. In no time she'd winkled the whole story out of Scarlett: Gemma's betrayal, the other girls' behaviour and the ongoing cold war they were waging. Scarlett knew the girls would have seen this as tale-telling, but she suddenly felt in real need of a sympathetic ear.

Miss Kitty *was* sympathetic, although she conceded that it might not have been wise to make entertainment of her friends' mannerisms in the first place. However, she agreed with Scarlett, it was hardly a heinous crime and well time they got over it. 'If they can't, then you must rise above it, my dear,' Miss Kitty advised her.

'I have tried,' Scarlett told her sadly.

Miss Kitty had worked for a short while in a boys' boarding school as the cook-cum-matron and had been the confidante of many bullied little boys. She told Scarlett what she often told them. 'I'm going to give you a piece of advice now, which you must swear never to share with a single living soul. Do I have your solemn word on that?' Scarlett nodded solemnly and Kitty leaned forward and whispered two words in her ear.

Scarlett broke out into a huge wide grin. It was exactly the advice she needed and there was no fear of her repeating it, especially at home, where she knew exactly what her mum's response would be – 'Scarlett Lee! Wash out your mouth!'

Thinking of her mum, Scarlett suddenly realised how late it was getting. As she left, Miss Kitty gave her some more uplifting words to help her on her way. 'Remember, Scarlett. This above all: to thine own self be true, And it must follow, as the night the day...' Scarlett, who'd heard this quotation many times before, joined in: 'Thou canst not then be false to any man.'

They were Miss Kitty's favourite lines from *Hamlet* and Scarlett was glad to be reminded of them. She left feeling a lot more cheerful than when she'd arrived.

When she got home Gerry's car was parked outside and Scarlett went in to find Gerry and her mum sitting at the kitchen table with a glass of wine each. There was an empty bottle on the worktop, and a second one already opened. Scarlett's mum wasn't usually much of a wine drinker; she was looking rather pink and giggly.

'Hello, darling,' she said, in a very odd voice.

There was no mention of Scarlett being home late from school. When she apologised her mum seemed surprised.

'Goodness, how's it got to that time?' her mother asked, a little too loudly. She kept on grinning and Gerry was grinning a lot too, Scarlett noticed.

'I brought you another present,' he said.

'Wasn't that kind?' said her mum, pushing it towards her. 'Another DDV.'

Gerry and her mum laughed again, even though it didn't seem particularly funny to Scarlett. She thought they were both behaving very oddly.

The DVD was an animated version of *Othello*.

'That's great,' said Scarlett. 'Is there anything to eat?' she asked pointedly, because there was no sign of any meal on the table, just almost-empty bowls of peanuts and crisps that Gerry offered in Scarlett's direction. Her mum got up to refill them, swayed a little and had to sit down again, which gave rise to another burst of laughter from her and Gerry.

Scarlett had never seen her mum like this before and didn't like it. Of course, it was nice to see her mum laughing for a change. But even so...

'Where's Cleo?' Scarlett asked.

'Upstairs,' said Mum grinning. 'She's got the humph.'

Scarlett assumed her mum meant *hump*. 'Nothing new there, then,' she commented.

'Aw, bless her,' said Mum, going all soppy for a moment. 'It's awful being an adolescent. I wouldn't want to go there again.'

'Oh, I don't know,' said Gerry. 'It had its moments.'

'She's far too *serious*,' Mum said, slurring the word. 'At least we had a bit more fun.'

'You certainly had plenty, as I remember,' Gerry commented.

Scarlett looked surprised. She didn't realise her

mum had known Gerry when they were teenagers.

'Your mum, I'll have you know,' Gerry told Scarlett, 'was the hottest girl in town.'

This caused Scarlett's mum to start giggling again and turn even pinker. It caused Scarlett to roll her eyes with embarrassment. She was tempted to leave them to it, but it occurred to Scarlett that if she stayed she might get some useful tips for the drunken scene in the play. She sat down and studied them both.

'You didn't know I went out with your mum first, did you?' Gerry asked Scarlett. 'She broke my heart.' He clutched his hand to it, as though it were still fragile. 'Like a fool I introduced her to your dad and he stole her from me.'

Her mum cocked her head to one side and gave Gerry a tipsy smile.

'Aw,' she said and patted his hand.

'I'm serious, I never recovered,' Gerry said again, with feeling. 'He always was a lucky devil.' He picked up the bottle and refilled both their glasses. Scarlett's mother tried to cover hers but was just too late. She shrugged and then reached for the bowl of crisps, almost knocking her glass over.

Scarlett groaned, reciting aloud one of Cassio's lines

in the play, after he gets drunk and regrets it: *'God that men should put an enemy in their mouths to steal away their brains.'*

Her mum and Gerry looked at her and started laughing hysterically. It was now getting *far* too embarrassing for Scarlett and she decided to leave them to their wine.

Upstairs she went to get her sister's opinion on the situation; it was pretty predictable.

'Disgusting!' Cleo announced. 'Utterly nauseating.'

Scarlett thought this was a shade over the top. 'They're just tipsy,' she said.

But Cleo wasn't prepared to dismiss it so lightly. 'I'll bet he deliberately set out to get her drunk,' she said, adding pointedly, 'While the cat's away...'

'What are you talking about?' Scarlett asked her.

'Oh, don't tell me you haven't noticed,' Cleo said, bitterly. 'You can't be blind as well as stupid. He's never away from here. He might as well move in.'

What on earth did she mean? Gerry...and their mum? Scarlett was open-mouthed; it was too ridiculous for words. What on earth had put that idea into her sister's brain? Scarlett looked more closely at Cleo.

'You should really get your head examined,' Scarlett told her. 'I mean *seriously*.'

Scarlett got out of her school uniform and straight into her pyjamas. She was hungry but she didn't want to go downstairs again. She just wanted to hide in her bedroom. She was furious with Cleo for even suggesting such a horrible idea and then putting it into Scarlett's head, where it had no place to be!

This must be what it's like for Othello, she thought, when Iago starts to plant his little lies. At first he *knows* that it's nonsense; he has faith in Desdemona. But then in no time – the space of one act – he's starting to wonder. After that the damage is done. Wherever he looks he sees more bits of evidence and slowly his doubts grow.

Scarlett shuddered. Well, that kind of thing might happen in a play, but this was real life, *her* family, *her* mum, for goodness sake. What was Cleo thinking of? Scarlett had a good mind to go back in and tell Cleo she was stark-staring bonkers.

Well, *she* wouldn't make the same mistakes as *Othello*. Scarlett wasn't going to believe stupid lies. She'd put them out of her mind now, once and for all.

But despite her best resolution, Scarlett had a lot of trouble putting them out of her mind and she spent a long time tossing and turning before she could get to sleep. So at breakfast the next morning she wasn't her usual bright-eyed and bushy-tailed self. When she came down there was a big row already raging between Cleo and her mum about the fact that Gerry's car was still parked outside their house!

'So where did *he* sleep?' Cleo demanded.

'In his own bed, I should hope,' Jenny replied.

'How come his car is still outside, then?' Cleo asked triumphantly.

'Because, Cleo, if it's any business of yours, Gerry got a taxi home last night. He doesn't drink and drive. He's a responsible sort of person.'

Cleo looked a little flattened by this information, but still not happy.

'And I hope you're not implying what I think you're implying,' her mum said in a quiet, measured voice.

Cleo looked away, a little ashamed, and left the kitchen.

Scarlett grinned and gave her mum a vigorous hug, which made Jenny wince. She was clearly suffering from a terrible hangover after all that unaccustomed wine. Scarlett made a mental note that when she grew up she would never put anything in her mouth to steal *her* brains away.

'Really,' she sighed, 'you'd think adults would know better.'

Chapter Thirteen

Exit, pursued by a bear.

Against all probability, Scarlett raced home every day that week in case her dad called. There had been no contact with him for over two weeks, since he'd left the Cap Verde islands. They still hadn't received a single postcard and Scarlett was really missing him. She knew that her mum and Cleo were too, but Scarlett was really, *really* missing him.

On Tuesday morning at breakfast it didn't help Scarlett's peace of mind when Cleo announced that she'd been trawling the internet and discovered all the things that could have gone wrong with the ship, from becoming becalmed in the Sargasso Sea, to hurricanes, illness, shipwreck – even pirate attack! Scarlett hadn't realised until then that pirates still existed.

'Something terrible's happened, I just know it,' Scarlett wailed. 'Do they still make people walk the plank? Dad could be fish food by now! We're never going to see him again!'

'You are such a fantasist,' Cleo told her.

Scarlett smiled briefly, as if this might be a compliment – which is certainly not what Cleo intended.

Their mum tried to reassure them both that if there had been any serious mishap they would have been informed by the emergency services by now. The yacht still had access to those, even if its other communication systems had broken down.

Scarlett, however, went to school in far from her usual high spirits. It was so much more difficult for her that she had no one to share any of it with. But their mum had already impressed on both the girls that until their dad was back in touch, they mustn't talk to *anyone*, especially about the police visits, because if people heard rumours it could harm his business.

Not that there was anyone Scarlett could share things with these days, she thought bitterly. She had never felt so completely alone, although she thought she might have detected some signs that the other girls were finally beginning to tire of trying to wind her up.

They had now reached the stage in rehearsals when they all realised that they needed to pull together. None of the girls were actually scared of their teacher; they all knew that his bark was much worse than his bite. But the shouting and pulling at his hair was getting extreme and everyone did their best to avoid upsetting Mr Coe.

Today it was Scarlett's turn to feel the full force of his frustration.

'For goodness' sake, Scarlett, you're not even thinking about the words. Can you please engage your brain – provided you can still locate it? Where is the emotion? If you don't *feel* it, Scarlett, there's no point trying to fake it.'

She tried not to let any of this upset her, but it was difficult. By now everyone else seemed to be settling into their roles, even Brogan, who had at last found a way to play Desdemona that wasn't too much at odds with her own feminist principles. The turning point had come when Brogan started wearing the wig in rehearsals. It was astonishing how it not only changed how she looked but even the way she delivered her lines. Scarlett heartily wished she had a wig that could magically transform her into Iago.

After her dressing-down from Mr Coe, Scarlett was surprised to see Gemma giving her what she thought might even be a sympathetic smile.

Another hopeful sign came a little later, during a short break in the rehearsal, when the girls started a heated discussion about which character was really responsible for the heap of dead bodies on the bed at the end of the play.

'It's all very well to keep blaming Iago and saying what a bad lot he is,' Brogan said to Abbie, 'but *you* have to take some of the blame.'

'Me?' said Abbie, only half-listening because she was busy plaiting her ponytail. 'What did I do?'

'You give Iago the stupid handkerchief. Why would you do that?'

'Yeah, if you didn't do that...' Leah joined in.

'Well, if you didn't behave like such a idiot and get plastered,' Abbie turned on Leah, 'Othello wouldn't sack you and listen to all Iago's stupid lies.'

'She's right,' Brogan agreed. 'People who can't hold their drink should stay out of the pub.'

Leah wasn't letting Brogan get away with that. 'Listen, if Desdemona wasn't such a wimp she'd stand up to Othello. She'd tell him he's being a five-star fool, believing all that garbage in the first place.'

'Who are you calling a wimp?' Brogan demanded, taking the insult entirely personally. 'I don't even *know* he's been fed all that *garbage*. And as for her!' she turned to Gemma. 'She's the biggest fool of all.'

Gemma blinked and said nothing.

'That's right,' Abbie agreed with Brogan. 'If Roderigo had taken no for an answer...'

'And not got tangled up with Iago and done his dirty work for him...' Leah added.

'Then none of this would have happened in the first place,' Abbie concluded.

Gemma just rolled her eyes and refused to get into the conversation. Her character was meant to be a fool. Surely everyone knew that.

But Scarlett couldn't keep quiet any longer. 'I think Othello's the biggest fool of all. Why would he believe Iago's lies? I mean...the evidence is pathetic!'

The girls turned to stare at her, as if she was a mute person who had suddenly started to speak. They seemed undecided whether or not to freeze her out again, but Brogan said, 'She's right. It's all because Othello's such a lame-brain.'

Zara sat nearby looking rather self-satisfied. Hers was the only character that was blameless in all this business. For the first time she felt pleased to be playing Bianca. 'I think you're all a pack of idiots,' she announced grandly.

There was suddenly a small round of applause from Mr Coe, who had been listening without them realising. It was the first time the girls had seen a smile on his face in days.

'That was an excellent summing up,' he said. '*Responsibility* and where it lies – always a complex question. It's very convenient to blame Iago, but in this play – as in life – nobody's blameless.'

Scarlett found the girls once more looking in her direction, but this time there was a definite hint of embarrassment on their faces, particularly Gemma's. Scarlett wasn't sure that spring had exactly sprung, but she could at last see that winter might be over.

Before he let the girls go, Mr Coe set them a small exercise to do at home. He'd talked before about the usefulness to acting of physical tasks, things they could do with their hands during a scene to help them find a deeper connection with their characters. Tasks like kneading bread, polishing a table, brushing one's hair (Scarlett always smiled at this one).

'Next time you're in the kitchen with your mum,' he said, 'I want you to watch very closely when she's making pastry...'

'My mum don't make pastry,' Leah announced.

'OK, then, the way your dad sharpens a knife.'

'That's very sexist, Mr C,' Brogan quickly pointed out.

'Yes, yes,' he hastily apologised, trying to head off another debate with Brogan. 'Perhaps I should have said, watch the way your mum – or dad – mends a fuse or darns a pair of socks.'

Abbie said her mum never mended anything. 'She says life's too short to darn a sock.'

Mr Coe thanked Abbie for sharing but said he was sure they all understood the point he was trying to make.

Scarlett rolled her eyes. It seemed unfair to her that *she'd* been the one he'd accused of disengaging her brain!

When she came out of Drama Club, Scarlett was surprised to see Gerry sitting in his car across the road, waiting for her. She went over to meet him.

'Thought you might like a lift home,' he said.

'Thanks,' Scarlett said and got in the car.

As Gerry drove he told her he'd wanted a quiet word with her – on her own.

'What about?' she asked, her suspicions rising.

'Your mum really,' he said. 'I'm a bit worried about her. She says she's fine, but I just wanted to check. How's she really doing?'

Scarlett shrugged. 'OK.'

'It's hard on her, your dad being away for so long.' Scarlett couldn't disagree with that. 'And I know Cleo isn't always...happy about me calling round, so I don't like to come too often. But I promised your dad I'd make sure you were all OK.'

'We *are*,' Scarlett assured him.

'Have you heard from him?' Gerry suddenly asked.

'No,' said Scarlett, surprised. Surely Gerry knew that?

'I just wondered.' He went quiet for a while. 'Your dad disappeared for a while once before, you know.' Scarlett was confused. They may not know *exactly* where her dad was, but it wasn't like he'd *disappeared*.

'He had a sort of breakdown,' Gerry went on. 'Not exactly a breakdown. But no one knew where he was then, either.'

Scarlett hadn't heard this story before. She wondered why no one had ever mentioned it to her.

'He works too hard, that's the trouble, and he doesn't really deal with stress.' Scarlett knew that her dad had changed jobs a couple of times in the past because they were too stressful. But these days, when he was home, he seemed perfectly relaxed to her.

'I'd do anything for your dad; you know that, don't you? Anything. It wouldn't matter to me what other people said about him.'

Scarlett didn't know what he meant by that.

'Until he comes home, I'll be there if you need me,' Gerry told her. 'So, if you're worried about your mum – or anything else – you call me. OK?'

Scarlett nodded. She still wasn't sure what else to say.

They'd arrived outside her house, and Gerry said finally, 'It's important we all support your mum and don't do *anything* to upset her. Understand?'

Scarlett could finally see where all this was leading. She thought Gerry was going to give her a little lecture about not arguing with Cleo, but Gerry didn't even mention that.

'So you don't need to tell her what I've said about

your dad, you know. Best keep it to yourself. OK?'

Scarlett didn't feel comfortable with the idea of keeping things from her mum, but she didn't say that to Gerry. She just nodded. As they got out of the car he reached into the back seat and took out a bunch of flowers.

'Carry these in for your mum, will you?'

Scarlett took them and watched Gerry as he unloaded two carrier bags of shopping from the boot. For the first time she began to wonder: could Cleo possibly be right? Wine, food, flowers – was he trying to get in with their mum? What was it that Cleo had said, *while the cat's away...*?

Hmm. We'll see about that, Scarlett thought, gritting her teeth.

Gerry stayed all evening and Scarlett watched his every move. But he didn't do anything to make her in the least bit more suspicious. Either there was nothing going on, she thought, or Gerry was a *very good actor*. He was just being his usual, funny self. And she had to admit that when he was around making jokes and being silly her mum seemed much more relaxed.

He'd brought some pizzas to warm up, so her mum

didn't have to cook again – but no wine this time – and a DVD. After Cleo's warning from their mum she ate with them in a reasonably civilised way, but when they all sat down to watch the film she excused herself to do homework. Scarlett carefully positioned herself on the sofa between her mum and Gerry, just in case.

When Jenny asked Gerry how his wife, Patti, was, Scarlett's ears pricked up. She wondered how Patti felt about him always hanging out at their house instead of his own. But it seemed that she was away again, with the girls, this time on holiday in Florida.

'Why didn't you go with them?' Scarlett asked Gerry.

'Someone's got to stay at home and pay the bills,' he joked. 'Maybe when your dad's back I'll get a bit of time off.'

'You certainly look as if you could do with it,' her mum commented. 'You look exhausted.'

But, as usual, Gerry laughed this off and by the time he left, Scarlett had to admit that she'd probably misjudged him. He hadn't done or said anything to which even Cleo could have objected.

So why did Scarlett still feel uneasy?

When she went upstairs she was tempted to tell Cleo about her conversation with Gerry in the car. But as soon as she went into Cleo's room she knew it was a mistake.

Cleo was having one of her silent sulks and these could be even more scary than her outbursts of temper. When she looked up from her book and saw Scarlett coming through the door two icy blasts shot across the room in her sister's direction.

'Whooo,' Scarlett shivered. 'Sorry to disturb you, O, Witch of the North.'

'Go *away*,' growled Cleo, searching for a suitable missile. She kept a number of soft toys on the end of her bed and, grabbing a selection, took aim. They rained down on Scarlett, who squealed in mock horror – then exited, *pursued by a bear*...

Chapter Fourteen

Life is better with a little drama in it!

For the next couple of days, Scarlett managed to keep her doubts about Gerry to herself, but it wasn't easy. Most of the time she was able to convince herself it was just Cleo's nonsense. But at low points she found herself racing to the end of Fantasy Avenue, where her worst fears were waiting for her.

One of them involved her mum and dad splitting up. Scarlett imagined her mum disappearing into the sunset with Gerry, while her dad was locked up in prison – and she and Cleo were sent to live in a foster home where she was forced to share a bedroom with the Ice Queen from Hell. It was enough to give anyone nightmares.

Scarlett was struggling, too, about having to keep secrets from her mum. She hated to keep *anything* to herself. She was someone who had to spit things out – literally. If Scarlett had a mouthful of food she detested, she couldn't possibly swallow it – and it was the same with unpleasant thoughts.

I don't get SECRETS. I mean, what is the point? If it's something good – like a wicked present you've got for someone – then you just want to tell as many people as possible. OBVIOUSLY. And if it's something bad, you want to get rid of it – out of your head – as fast as you can. SIMPLE.

And it did seem that simple to Scarlett.

When she came home from Drama Club on Thursday her mum was in the kitchen listening to a CD and doing the ironing. There was the pleasant smell of freshly ironed clothes and Scarlett was glad to see her mother looking a little more relaxed. Maybe now was Scarlett's chance to ask her a few leading questions.

She sighed dramatically, casting her bag and coat around the kitchen.

'I'm *starving*,' she groaned, and turning herself into Oliver Twist begged, 'Please sir, can I have some *food*...'

Her mother smiled. 'Dinner'll be half an hour at least; you know where the fridge is. How did rehearsals go?' she asked in a routine kind of way.

Scarlett shrugged, 'OK.' She got herself a drink, some biscuits and a banana. Then she proceeded to dunk her biscuit in her drink and alternately eat a mouthful of banana and one of soggy biscuit. Her mother rolled her eyes and went back to the ironing.

Scarlett stared thoughtfully at her mum. She was aware that her mum was pretty, that she wore nice clothes – for her age, anyway – and had lovely curly hair that Cleo had inherited but sadly Scarlett hadn't. But she never thought of her mum as *sexy*. Just the word – in relation to *her mum* – made Scarlett want to giggle.

Her parents often had a little kiss or a cuddle in front of Scarlett and Cleo, but not that sloppy embarrassing stuff you saw on TV, thank goodness. She'd never seen her mum flirting with anyone else; she wouldn't do it. Scarlett just knew that about her mum. And yet... A nagging little voice reminded her she thought she had known everything about her dad, too, but Gerry had proved her wrong.

'You're very thoughtful,' her mum remarked.

Scarlett sighed again, as if coming out of a daydream. She knew she should probably bring the subject up casually, skirt around it for a while, but she ended up just plunging in: 'Did dad once have a nervous breakdown?'

'Where on earth did that come from?' her mum asked, frowning and shaking her head.

Scarlett didn't want to dump Gerry in it. 'Just something I overheard.'

'You can't possibly remember it; you were only a baby. '

'Yes, but did he?'

'Not really. He had a stressful job at the time, and spent long hours commuting into London. Suddenly we had two little children and it all got on top of him. That's all.'

'Did he disappear?'

'For a few days.'

'Why didn't you ever tell me about it?' Scarlett asked, accusingly.

Her mum shrugged. 'It was a long time ago.'

Scarlett still wished she'd known. But her mum was looking at her suspiciously, so she changed the subject. 'Why did you choose Dad instead of Gerry?'

'Good heavens,' her mum laughed. 'What is this, the hot seat?'

'Just asking,' Scarlett said, defensively.

'I suppose Dad was more reliable, steadier.'

'You make him sound like a car. Surely you loved Dad more?' asked Scarlett.

'Of course I did. But there are lots of other factors when you're deciding who to spend the rest of your life with. Gerry was a real charmer – and lots of fun,' her mother said, smiling. 'He could always make me laugh. But he never had any money and he still hasn't. He didn't like working hard. When they were at school, your dad always did his homework for him. He just wasn't someone you'd want to depend on...your dad was.'

Scarlett wrinkled up her nose, visualising her dad as a big old family car – reliable but a little bit boring – and Gerry as a cool blue sports car, just like the one he drove.

Her mum started to reminisce about those old days and Scarlett tuned in and out as she watched her doing the ironing.

'I suppose you can't help wondering sometimes:

what if you'd made different choices...' her mother said.

'What kind of choices?' Scarlett wanted to know.

Her mum blinked, 'Oh...if we'd stayed living in London...if we'd never had children...'

'Never had *us*?' Scarlett said, horrified.

'I know...unthinkable, isn't it?' her mum teased. 'But say I'd never met your dad...say Gerry had never introduced us...say I'd married Gerry...'

Scarlett swallowed hard. This was not the way she wanted the conversation to go. She couldn't bring herself to look at her mum's face, so she concentrated all her attention on Jenny's hands ironing their school shirts. Scarlett suddenly thought about Mr Coe's exercise: to carefully observe ordinary actions.

She found herself imitating her mum's movements with the iron, trying to *feel* the action. She watched Jenny bend to take out a few more items from the basket. Now she was ironing a handkerchief. She turned it over, folded it, folded it again, pressed it lightly. Scarlett recognised Gerry's initials in the corner. It was the handkerchief he'd lent Jenny a week ago, when she'd got upset after the second police visit.

Her mum was still talking: about Gerry, about Dad, about how life might have been different. She gave the handkerchief a small, almost tender little pat, before she laid it aside.

Something that had only been niggling at the very back of Scarlett's brain now seemed to be straining for her attention. Suddenly, like a crucial piece in a jigsaw, it fell into place. It had to be a sign, a clue. Scarlett knew – in her very bones – that Cleo was right: Gerry was still after their mum. He hadn't been able to keep her all those years ago but, now their dad had stupidly gone away and left the path clear, he was determined to get her back.

Scarlett started to feel sick. Ignoring the fact that her mum was still talking to her, she got up and raced upstairs.

'Just need the bathroom,' she called back by way of explanation.

For a few minutes Scarlett hid in there until she felt a bit calmer. She couldn't go back downstairs and face her mum yet. She knew she would probably blurt it all out like an idiot if she did. But she couldn't stay in there, on her own with these horrible thoughts. She had to share them with someone, which meant she'd have to swallow her pride and tell Cleo that she'd been right all along. It was going to stick in Scarlett's throat to admit it, but it had to be done.

Once Scarlett had relayed to Cleo her conversation in the car with Gerry – and the vital clue of the handkerchief – the sisters were united. The double-crossing, wife-stealing Gerry and what to do about him became their common cause.

'I knew it! I knew it!' Cleo announced, stamping around the bedroom. She told Scarlett she'd made the right decision not to discuss it with their mum and to come to her instead. Both girls seemed to have formed the same picture of their mum as the innocent party who, until their dad came back, needed protecting – clearly by them.

They agreed that under no circumstances would they ever leave their mum and Gerry alone together. They – especially Cleo – wouldn't arouse any more suspicion by being rude or cold towards him, but neither would they be exactly friendly. They would let him know, in all sorts of subtle ways, that they were on to him.

'Men!' Cleo ranted. 'I wouldn't trust one as far as I could throw him. Cheats and liars, all of them, Dad excepted, of course. It's pathetic: all the corny ways he's been trying to seduce Mum with flowers and food and wine!'

Seduce was Cleo's word and Scarlett didn't like it. It made things sound more real and serious than Scarlett privately hoped they were.

But Cleo was ready to believe even worse of Gerry. 'I wouldn't put it past *him* to have been cooking the books all along, and planning a disappearing act with Mum, using Dad's money! I'll bet he's already stashed it away and bought the tickets!' she said.

Scarlett almost laughed out loud. It was too ridiculous. She might just be able to believe that Gerry was a bit of a love-rat, but this was like Cleo's other conspiracy theories about government and big business controlling the whole world for their own ends.

Cleo was going completely over the top. Scarlett looked pityingly at her sister and observed to herself, 'And *I'm* supposed to be the Drama Queen!'

Chapter Fifteen

The plot thickens...

When Drama Club met on the following Tuesday – with only days to go before the first performance – everyone's anxiety was running high, not least Mr Coe's. Scarlett was a little concerned about him. She couldn't believe that getting so angry was good for his health.

Scarlett didn't know Mr Coe's age, but she suspected he looked a good deal older than he really was. As well as his thinning hair, he had a little potbelly and a bit of a double chin. He didn't look like he ate very healthy food.

The teacher had been raking his hair and ranting at the girls for several minutes without drawing breath. Scarlett was tempted to tell him, 'Chill, *chill*, Mr C. Go with the flow...' But she suspected that right now he wouldn't take it in the spirit it was intended.

'In case you've all forgotten, it's only *two days* to the final rehearsal, three days to the first performance!' he announced. 'We've still got an impossible amount to sort out. This is promising to be a disaster of mammoth proportions!'

But when Mr Coe did finally stop ranting and registered the girls' terrified faces, he sighed deeply, left his hair alone and completely switched tactics.

'The most important thing is for everyone to stay *calm* and *open*,' he said, in as calm a voice as he could manage. 'Everything's going to be fine. Apart from one or two small details you're all doing just...*fine*. A little more work and this could still be your best performance yet.'

He directed the girls to lie down, close their eyes and completely relax for five minutes. Meanwhile Mr Coe paced the floor, trying to control his own mounting anxiety. It was nothing new for the girls to hear their teacher say one thing and do the opposite.

But their relaxation was soon disturbed by the arrival of Mr Coe's son, Damion, and Damion's friend, Leon. Mr Coe had asked them to come in to video one or two of the scenes in rehearsal. They were also going to be doing the lighting and sound for the play.

But two adolescent boys, albeit a little spotty and geeky, were such a rare sight in an all girls' school that it entirely unsettled everyone. Zara flirted shamelessly and as usual most of the other girls followed her lead.

Brogan didn't join in. She had her own strong feelings about the boys being there; she'd already shared these with Mr Coe on other occasions.

'We don't need *boys*! You said I could do the techy jobs. Last time you *promised*. It ain't fair, Mr C,' she huffed and puffed.

But Mr Coe reminded Brogan that she had a vital role already and said that, despite her many talents, there was no way she could play Desdemona and control the lighting. Brogan glared at the boys throughout the session.

Scarlett didn't like the boys being there, either. Damion with his bare feet and leggings, and Leon with his pathetic, wispy beard that looked as if he'd found it at the bottom of a very old make-up box, were trying far too hard to look like drama students, and Scarlett found them deeply embarrassing.

So it wasn't surprising that the video hardly gave a fair picture of the girls' performances. When Mr Coe played it back, they couldn't stop giggling and pointing. Some had been almost paralysed by the presence of the camera *and* the boys, while others, notably Scarlett and Zara, had badly over-acted.

It was a bit of a wake-up call to Scarlett, who had been quite hopeful that she was getting to grips with Iago's complex character. Seeing herself on film, she realised how wrong she'd been. No one would have mistaken her Iago as an *honest* man; she was still playing him as a pantomime villain. Why was it so much harder to play a villain pretending to be a nice guy, than a villain honestly being a bad one, she wondered?

Scarlett could tell Mr Coe was disappointed with her and it gave her no comfort that the other girls weren't doing any better. She again felt deeply frustrated that all those wonderful death scenes were going to waste on Eve and Brogan and Abbie. If only Scarlett had a long, lingering death to get her teeth into she knew she'd be doing better.

At the end of the session, Mr Coe confirmed Scarlett's fears when he suggested that she might need to give up a couple of break times to work with him on her soliloquies. Scarlett went home feeling completely crushed.

*

At the end of yet another really bad day, all Scarlett wanted when she got home was a little attention from her mum – and perhaps a bit of sympathy. She was sorely disappointed.

Gerry was there and, despite her hanging round the kitchen looking sad and listless, even he was giving Scarlett no attention either.

'Haven't you got some homework to do?' Mum asked, rather sharply.

Scarlett couldn't deny that she had. She went upstairs to make a start, but met Cleo on the landing.

'Where do you think you're going?'

Scarlett blinked at her in confusion. 'To my bedroom?' she said.

But Cleo shook her head and turned her sister back the way she'd come.

'We never leave them on their own,' she reminded Scarlett.

'Oh, can't you do it?' Scarlett groaned, but Cleo propelled her back downstairs.

'Pretend you're a spy,' Cleo whispered. 'It'll be good acting practice.'

Hmm, that made it a little more attractive, Scarlett thought.

Back in the kitchen, she smiled artificially at her mum and made some excuse about her room being a mess, which was only half a lie. She set her books out on the kitchen table and settled down to her biology homework.

But, as if they were trying to get away from Scarlett, her mum and Gerry moved through to the lounge.

Scarlett felt obliged to follow them. 'In case I need some help,' she said, lamely.

Scarlett opened her homework diary and headed the page: *Spy Notes*.

She wrote number one, but waited in vain for anything worth recording.

She tried to pay attention to her mum and Gerry's conversation, but it was about boring grown-up stuff like money and bills – *yawn, yawn* – nothing useful she could report back to Cleo. Within minutes Scarlett was so bored she thought she might scream. She really began to think that she and Cleo had imagined it all.

She was so relieved when Gerry said he had to leave that she almost cheered. Patti and the girls were due home the next day and he wanted to get the house cleaned up, he explained. 'I've been living like a student for two weeks and I need to dispose of the evidence.'

As they were seeing Gerry out, Scarlett slipped her arm through her mum's, already laying claim to her attention. But she was once more to be disappointed. Another car had drawn up with more visitors: DI Maddox and PC Dryer.

'Here *again*, Mr Thomas?' DI Maddox said, as he passed Gerry in the driveway. Scarlett thought this sounded a bit rude, but Cleo gave Scarlett a look that clearly said, you see, even the police have noticed!

'We just have a few more questions we need to ask,' they told Jenny. 'I don't suppose your husband's been in touch yet?'

Jenny shook her head. 'I told you I'd ask him to contact you the moment he does.'

'Yes, well, we hope he will,' he said rather formally. 'But, in the meantime, we're still making our own attempts to contact him. If I could perhaps speak to you in private?'

Once more Scarlett and Cleo had to content

themselves with waiting in the hall with PC Dryer. Scarlett was entertained by watching the young policeman trying to make conversation with Cleo about school, her exams, and, finally in desperation, her trainers. But Cleo studiously ignored him.

Suddenly the door opened. DI Maddox walked out as he asked their mum, 'And you'll treat everything I've said as *strictly* confidential?'

She nodded her head and deliberately avoided the girls' eyes.

'Thank you,' he said.

PC Dryer tried one last time to get a smile from Cleo, but she gave him such an icy glare the poor boy almost reeled back from the force of it.

'Idiots!' Cleo muttered, even before her mum had closed the door.

Jenny grabbed Cleo by the arm and led her forcibly into the kitchen. 'What has got into you?' she demanded. 'How dare you show me up like that?' All the while she kept hold of Cleo's arm.

'I'm sick of them harassing us,' Cleo said, shaking her off. 'They ought to have better things to do with their time. You'd think Dad had committed some terrible crime!'

There was a short silence while the girls both waited for their mum to deny this. When she didn't, Cleo asked, 'Well, has he?' Scarlett held her breath, but their mother still said nothing.

'Why won't you tell us what's going on?' Cleo demanded. 'We're not babies.'

Scarlett opened her mouth to join in, but her mum put up her hand.

'Don't!' she warned. She sat down at the kitchen table, shaking her head. 'It's all been some silly mistake. It's nothing you need to be worried about.'

'How can it be nothing?!' Cleo demanded to know. 'What were you talking about in there?'

But their mother was evasive. 'Just stuff about the business.'

'Why don't they ask Gerry all that? Why do they keep coming here?'

'It's complicated,' Jenny shrugged.

'Something's going on, I know it,' Cleo insisted. 'Why won't you tell us?'

Their mum looked on the point of tears and Scarlett went to put her arm round her. 'Leave her alone,' she told Cleo.

But Cleo and Jenny just kept staring at each other

until Jenny finally admitted, 'OK, there's some money gone missing, from the business, from clients' accounts – a lot of money. They're investigating for fraud.'

'And they think Dad's done it?'

'No, no, they don't...'

'Then why do they keep coming here?'

'Because it's Dad's business; he has overall responsibility.'

'But Gerry said it was nothing – just routine. VAT and *stuff*...' Cleo looked and sounded frantic now.

'Well, perhaps he's wrong.'

'Surely not! The wonderful Gerry!'

'For goodness' sake,' their mother exploded. 'I've had enough of this nonsense, Cleo.' She narrowed her eyes at Cleo, challenging her to say more, but Cleo couldn't bring herself to admit what she knew, deep down, were probably exaggerated fears.

'I'm finding your behaviour very hard to handle. When *anyone* comes to this house I expect you to show them some respect, whether it's Gerry or the police. Do I make myself clear?' Mum asked.

Cleo gave the slightest nod.

'You really need to get your temper under control,

Cleo. You're behaving like a...a shrew.'

Cleo stood there, silenced, but unbowed.

Her mum's description of her sister made Scarlett want to laugh out loud.

She struggled to get her face under control as Cleo turned to leave the kitchen. She knew that in Cleo's present mood even a smile would be like a red rag to a bull.

Scarlett thought that she had finally got her mum to herself, so when the doorbell rang again almost immediately, she let out a howl of frustration. Cleo yanked the front door almost off its hinges in her temper, which wasn't improved when she saw who was there. She stepped aside to allow Gerry to pass but slammed the door behind him. Cleo stomped upstairs shouting, 'It's like flaming Piccadilly Circus in here!'

Jenny shook her head and asked Scarlett to put on the kettle.

Scarlett made a pot of tea then hovered in the kitchen, reluctantly chaperoning her mum and Gerry once more.

'I thought I'd better come back and see what they wanted *this* time,' Gerry explained.

Scarlett noticed that her mum was hardly even

looking at Gerry. She clearly wasn't in the mood for any more visitors. But she poured two cups of tea, passed Gerry his and then walked into the lounge. When Scarlett tried to follow, her mum said, 'Stay!' in a tone that made Scarlett feel like the family dog! 'I'd like *you* to get on with your homework now,' her mum added.

Scarlett sat down again in the kitchen and settled for eavesdropping.

'I've been over the accounts,' she heard Gerry tell her mum, 'and I can't see any explanation for the missing money. Did they say how much was involved?'

'No,' her mother said, 'but it's clearly a lot.'

There was a silence then and Scarlett got up to look through the crack in the door. Her mum had her head in her hands, as if she were crying. Gerry moved closer to her and put his hand on her back.

Scarlett's heart was racing. She was praying nothing was about to happen that she might need to make a note of! Relief flooded over her as her mum held up her hand, and flinched.

'Don't, please. I'm fine,' she whispered and Gerry moved away again.

Things went quiet for a while and Scarlett could only

pick out odd words. She realised how vital good hearing was to a spy. There couldn't be much work for a deaf spy, she thought, although lip-reading would have been a very useful skill right now.

'I don't understand how this can be happening!' her mum suddenly exploded.

'There's got to be a good explanation,' Gerry said, trying to calm her.

'Like what! That Steve's done it? Stolen the money and disappeared?' her mum asked. It made Scarlett's blood run cold. She could see her mum calmly looking into Gerry's face, demanding an answer.

'No, absolutely not.' Gerry shook his head. 'I'll never accept that.'

'Neither will I,' her mum agreed. 'But I think the police believe he's run off to South America or somewhere.'

'That's ridiculous,' Gerry said. 'You don't think that, do you?'

Scarlett was desperate to hear her mum's reply. She had to lean forward to catch it.

'No, of course not,' she said quietly. 'Steve wouldn't do a thing like that. He'll be in touch any day now and then the truth will come out.'

Scarlett felt reassured by her mum's words, but not by Gerry's reply.

'I hope so, Jenny. I really hope you're right.'

When Gerry left, he didn't even say goodbye to Scarlett. She thought he looked a bit odd, as if he hadn't slept for a week. Was that how worried he was about Dad's business? Scarlett felt a bit guilty. Over the last month she'd thought about her dad lots, but she'd been so caught up with her own troubles, she'd not exactly lost any sleep over him.

Scarlett had so many questions she wanted to ask, but she didn't want to upset her mum any more, so she went upstairs and left Jenny in peace. She crept past her sister's bedroom door – she didn't want to talk to Cleo right now.

Scarlett was sure of one thing at least: there was no way on this planet her dad could have done anything bad, like stealing other people's money. It wasn't in his nature. Her dad had a conscience; he cared about people. He gave money to charity. He was a good person. Scarlett knew that; she just *knew* it.

But that mean little voice inside her head reminded her that she wasn't always quite as good at judging other people as she liked to think. Look at the business with Gemma. Scarlett hadn't seen that coming, had she? She'd thought she knew her friend inside out, but she'd got Gemma completely wrong. Spineless? Scarlett didn't think so – not any more!

She'd probably got Gerry wrong, too. She'd been so quick to agree with Cleo and believe the worst of him: all that rubbish about him being after their mum! It was much more likely that he'd just been keeping his promise to her dad to look after them all. She should never have let Cleo draw her into her own silly suspicions.

I don't know how you can ever be COMPLETELY SURE about anyone else. Mr Coe says the way to understand another person is to get inside their skin – TO LOOK BEHIND THE MASK. But, surely, not everyone wears a mask. I don't, and I don't think Dad wears one…or Mum…not even Cleo (except when she plays The Ice Queen).

At least I hope they don't. That would be too scary to think about.

For once writing it all down wasn't helping very much and Scarlett was still left in a terrible mood. She absolutely ached to have her dad home. As big as she was, Scarlett just wanted to climb on his knee. It was so long since she'd last seen him, she was starting to worry that she might be forgetting what he looked like.

Usually, there was nothing she liked better than creating a bit of a scene, having a good outburst, being the Queen of Drama Queens. But that was when there wasn't much at stake, when her life was going along normally. This was different. This felt SERIOUS.

Now all she wanted to do was hide in her room. She didn't want anyone to see how scared she was feeling. Or how much she was truly hurting.

She hid her face in her pillow and let the tears come.

Some things, even Scarlett realised, weren't meant to have an audience.

Chapter Sixteen

Something wicked this way comes.

After the dramas of the previous night, it seemed extraordinary to Scarlett that life should carry on as normal the next morning, but her mum had gone to work and she and Cleo had gone to school. Gerry had called round in the evening, as usual, but he wasn't offered a cup of tea and he hadn't stayed long. In fact, Scarlett thought her mum seemed a bit cool with him, but then she was being cool with her and Cleo too. But when she mentioned this to Cleo, her sister had sighed, 'What do you expect? Mum's under a lot of strain.'

Scarlett felt that she was under a lot of strain, too. She'd had another miserable day at school. Mr Coe was still raking his hair in frustration and reminding them, as if they needed any reminder, that tomorrow was the dress rehearsal, with the first performance on Friday, and still no one was word perfect!

Nor had there been any phone call from their dad, even though this was the week he'd been expected to reach the Caribbean and make contact with them.

On a more positive note, Cleo was being nicer to Scarlett. In fact she was giving a very good impersonation of a protective older sister. They were both sitting now on Cleo's bed and Scarlett had finally started to confide in her sister all about Gemma and the trouble she'd been having with her friends in Drama Club.

Cleo listened sympathetically, but she couldn't resist reminding Scarlett that she'd tried to warn her where all that mimicking was going to lead. 'Never mind, they'll get over it,' Cleo said. 'Girls always do, eventually.'

Scarlett sighed deeply. She still *honestly* couldn't see that she'd done anything very bad, but she'd finally had to that accept this wasn't how her friends probably saw it.

Before she went to bed, Scarlett came very close to ringing Gemma; she actually picked up the phone. But then she thought: if Gemma *had* got over herself and they became friends again, how would Scarlett manage to keep the horrible secrets about her dad to herself? She put the phone down and went off to bed instead, trying to follow Cleo's advice not to think about it.

Scarlett lay on her bed trying instead to focus her attention on the play, but the thought of the next day's final rehearsal, something that would normally have filled her with excitement, now only filled her with dread. It was a new and unwelcome feeling for Scarlett. She fell into a light, fitful sleep and woke the next morning feeling tired and out of sorts.

Scarlett had a nasty feeling she might have turned overnight into a typical teenager. Until recently she had always been an early riser with, in Cleo's view, a perfectly disgusting amount of energy at breakfast time. But this morning she didn't even want to get out of bed; she simply couldn't bear the thought of it.

Scarlett considered pulling a sickie. She'd never tried this before but, being such an accomplished actress, she was sure it would be a piece of cake to convince her mum that she was at death's door.

She lay in bed and imagined herself with food poisoning. She practised clutching her stomach while writhing in pain. But then she suspected her mum might expect her to actually vomit – a thing Scarlett absolutely hated.

She practised shivering instead and being burnt up with a phantom cold – maybe even full-blown flu. She added a hacking cough that she was confident would have her confined to bed for a week.

If all else failed, Scarlett could probably faint for England.

But no matter how tempting it all seemed, in the end she couldn't bring herself to let Mr Coe down. She knew he was depending on her, so she nobly dragged herself out of bed, ignoring the string of symptoms that seemed so convincing she was starting to believe them herself.

Scarlett raced into school late, passing Mr Coe in the corridor.

'You look awful, Scarlett. Are you ill?'

'No, sir,' Scarlett replied, thinking she'd obviously done too good a job.

'You haven't forgotten we're meeting up at break?' he asked.

Rats! Scarlett had forgotten, but she lied impressively. 'Of course not,' she said, her heart sinking. She sincerely wished she'd stayed in bed after all.

At break time, Scarlett struggled through her pieces.

'With such a little web as this I will trap such... a great spider as Cassio?' she said, hopefully.

'Close,' Mr Coe sighed. 'But *not* close enough. You lose all the poetry when you mangle the lines like that. And could we have it with more feeling next time? Come on, Scarlett,' he pleaded. 'You're just going through the motions.'

Scarlett would have preferred it if Mr Coe had raked through his hair and bawled her out. Instead she had to deal with that look of deep disappointment he sometimes wore, which was far worse. She looked away to avoid meeting his eye.

'The whole play depends on you, Scarlett. I just can't understand what's going on. I know this is a difficult part but you've risen to the challenge before. What's wrong? You can tell me.'

Scarlett came very close to pouring out all her worries, especially those about her dad, but she'd promised her mum. She numbly shook her head and admitted that maybe the part had been a bit hard to get into, but she thought she was getting there.

Mr Coe disagreed. 'I don't think you are, Scarlett. You don't seem to understand the complexity of Iago. You're still playing him as a one-dimensional baddie.'

Scarlett sighed.

'You need to understand him, even like him.'

'Why would anyone *like* him?' Scarlett snapped. 'He's horrible.'

'But people do. It's all there in the play. And the audience has to, at one level. He's a charmer. He knows how to seduce people.'

Scarlett blinked. That dreadful word again. 'I don't understand why no one sees through him,' she declared. 'I know I would have done. He wouldn't have charmed me!' she said with real anger.

'You say that, Scarlett, because you and the audience are in his confidence. But to the other characters in the play he wears an entirely different face: a decent, human face. It's only when he stops pretending...and the mask slips...that we see the real face of Iago.'

Scarlett rolled her eyes; she still didn't buy it.

'You don't believe that people wear different faces? That they can *seem* good but *be* bad?'

Scarlett shrugged. 'Maybe,' she conceded, 'but I think I'd *always* know the difference.'

She wasn't thinking about Iago now; she was thinking about her dad. There were some people you just knew you could be sure of and nothing Mr Coe said was going to shake that trust.

Mr Coe groaned. 'Well, I'm sorry to have to tell you, Scarlett, but life is not that simple. Sometimes we have to accept that things aren't always how they seem. Villains are complicated; they're rarely *all* bad.'

'Miss Kitty says they are,' Scarlett quickly replied. 'She says you can psychoanalyse Iago till the cows come home for milking and you still won't understand him.'

Mr Coe sighed. He was well used to Scarlett passing on her singing teacher's words of wisdom but today he didn't have the patience to be diplomatic.

'Well, it may not be Miss Kitty's reading of the play, but this is the one *I* want you to consider: it's pure envy that drives Iago to his extreme actions. He's continually faced with other people's power and good fortune and envy affects his judgement. He becomes corrupted by it and finds himself in a cycle that he can't break – even if he wanted to – one bad action leading to another.'

Scarlett pressed her lips together and let Mr Coe run on. She couldn't agree with the teacher just to please him, but she didn't want him to think she was being stubborn.

'Just think about what I've said, Scarlett,' he suggested, looking at his watch. 'And try to get your head into a better place before tonight. There's a lot to get through. It's our final rehearsal. I hope to goodness everyone's remembered their blacks. I promise you, anyone who hasn't will be for the high jump!'

A black top and leggings was their drama uniform, and Scarlett's heart sank even further when she realised she'd completely forgotten hers.

Mr Coe studied her. 'I hope you're not one of those people,' he said, ominously.

'No,' she said, brightly. 'They're in my bag.' Scarlett neglected to tell him that her bag was currently sitting on her bedroom floor at home. She left wondering how much worse the day could still get.

However disappointed Mr Coe felt with her, it was

nothing compared to Scarlett's own disappointment with herself. This forgetful, unmotivated, lazy person wasn't who she really was. She couldn't bear losing any more of Mr Coe's good opinion. She would just have to go home and get her clothes. She could manage it in the lunch hour at a push. She'd be back before anyone missed her.

There was just one problem. She would need to borrow Gemma's bike. Scarlett didn't look forward to asking Gemma a favour, but she was desperate. This was no time for misplaced pride.

During the next lesson – chemistry – Scarlett was so preoccupied she managed to get into Miss Whalley's bad books too.

'For goodness' sake, Scarlett, wake up and join us, please? I don't think you've taken in a single word I've said this morning.'

Scarlett tried to look apologetic. She noticed Gemma watching her and was surprised to see another sympathetic smile. This was all the encouragement she needed. Scarlett took the first chance she got to go over to Gemma, and deliver the little speech she'd been preparing.

'Look, Gemma, I need a favour. I know I've no right

to ask – I know we haven't been friends lately and I know that's probably my fault. I'm really, really sorry about all of it...'

There was more to come but Gemma cut her off. 'What kind of favour?'

'I need to borrow your bike. I forgot my blacks and I'm in mega-deep you-know-what with Mr Coe.'

'OK,' Gemma said, hardly glancing at her. Scarlett looked more closely at her, though. Gemma looked *very* pale.

'Are you OK?'

Gemma nodded. 'It's just the thought of the dress rehearsal. I still don't know my lines. I wish I'd never got this part. I should have listened to you; I should have stuck to a walk-on part. I feel like I'm going to be sick.'

Scarlett put her hand on Gemma's arm. 'I owe you for this. When I get back I'll help you with your lines. You're going to be fine, you know. You could do this standing on your head, balancing a teacup on your feet, reading the *Beano*.'

This was one of the girls' old jokes. Gemma looked up and smiled at Scarlett. Both girls clearly wanted to say a lot more, but they'd been friends long enough not to need to. Scarlett nodded and smiled back.

The minute the end-of-morning bell rang, Scarlett headed to the bike sheds and grabbed Gemma's bike. She pedalled as fast as she could. At least one thing had gone right today; now perhaps she and Gemma would sort out their quarrel and other things would start looking up.

Scarlett flew past the shops, the park and the garage. A short way from home, parked way down a side street, she saw a familiar blue sports car. She wondered if it was Gerry's, although as far as she knew he didn't have any other friends who lived close by.

Racing into her drive, Scarlett immediately realised that in her haste she'd forgotten to bring her house key. It was still in her locker, in her jacket pocket. *Idiot!* Scarlett told herself. She would have to use the spare; there was one always hidden under the big pot plant by the front door.

Scarlett felt around underneath it, but she couldn't find the key. She even heaved the pot aside. Scarlett groaned. It wasn't there. She had no time to ride back to school to pick hers up. The key was supposed to be there for exactly this kind of emergency!

Scarlett ran round the side of the house and tried the back door, in vain. She did a full circuit of the house, looking for an open window. It had been quite hot for the last week, and just maybe one had been left open. But no luck!

As she came back round the front of the house she walked past her dad's study window. Out of the corner of her eye Scarlett saw someone inside. For a split second she thought her dad was home! Her heart was suddenly bursting with excitement. But she soon saw that it was not her dad's face staring out at her; *it was Gerry's.*

It would have been difficult to say who looked the more surprised. For a horrible moment Scarlett wondered if her mum was at home, inside the house with Gerry. All those horrible suspicions flew back into her head. But Gerry came straight to the window, smiling at her.

'Do you want to come in?' he mouthed.

Scarlett made her way to the front door. At least she'd get her drama clothes now, but she couldn't think *what* Gerry was doing inside her house.

Gerry, however, didn't behave as if he was in

the least bit out of place. He held the door back, inviting her in as if this were his house and she was the visitor.

'You nearly gave me a heart attack,' he told her, cheerfully. 'You were the last person I expected to see staring through the window.'

Scarlett wanted to say, *But I'm the one who lives here!* Instead she found herself explaining why she was there. 'I had to get my things for the play...I left my key at school...the spare wasn't there...'

'No, I used it,' Gerry said. 'I needed to get in. Don't look worried. I can explain everything.' He closed the door and walked back into the study. Scarlett followed him – feeling slightly anxious.

'I've been digging around at work and there were some of your dad's papers I needed. I've just been trying to sort out this mess.' He turned to Scarlett. 'That's what we all want, isn't it?'

Scarlett nodded – it seemed to make sense.

'I'm just trying to get the police off our backs. I don't know how long we'd have to wait for Detective Dynamite and PC Plod to get to the bottom of it. Not the best set of brains on the planet,' he said, grinning.

Scarlett tried to grin back, but she found it difficult. It all sounded OK, so why was she feeling uncomfortable?

'Don't worry, we'll get to the bottom of it – you and me. What a team, hey?'

Scarlett couldn't imagine what *she* could do, but if there *was* anything she'd do it like a shot. Right now, though, she had to get her clothes and get back to school. She headed for the stairs.

'Do you need a lift back?' Gerry called after her.

'No, thanks,' she said. 'I've got Gemma's bike.'

Scarlett ran upstairs and into her bedroom. She grabbed what she needed and bundled it into a rucksack. She suddenly remembered seeing Gerry's car and was just wondering what it was doing parked a few streets away, when she heard the doorbell ring.

She stood on the landing and looked down the stairs. Gerry was standing in the hall, pressed back against the wall. He was making no attempt to answer the door. Instead he indicated to Scarlett to stay where she was.

Scarlett was puzzled and frowned at Gerry, but he waved her back, out of sight. Scarlett found herself stepping back, away from the view of anyone looking through the glass panel in the front door. What on earth was going on, she wondered? Who were they supposed to be hiding from?

The doorbell rang again. This was stupid. Scarlett moved back to the top of the stairs but Gerry furiously shook his head and mouthed, 'It's the police.' He waved his hand to indicate she shouldn't let them see her.

'Why?' Scarlett mouthed back. But Gerry just held up a warning finger.

A moment later whoever it was walked away, and Scarlett slowly went downstairs.

'Why didn't you let them in?' she asked.

'I've told you. The police aren't really on our side.'

'Our side?' Scarlett repeated.

Gerry looked at her for a long moment. He wasn't smiling now.

'I don't understand,' she said. 'What's going on?'

Gerry took a deep breath. 'OK, if you're really sure you want to know.'

The way Gerry said it, Scarlett wasn't sure she did, but she found herself nodding anyway.

'Let's go into the kitchen,' he said, taking her arm. 'You might need to sit down.'

Chapter Seventeen

I'll pour this pestilence into his ear...

Scarlett followed Gerry into the kitchen. He went straight to the kettle and started to make two cups of coffee.

'I haven't got time for a drink!' she told him. 'I have to get back. Like *now*!'

Gerry acknowledged he'd heard her but carried on making his own coffee. Scarlett realised she should have left already if she wanted to stay out of trouble at school. But Gerry was slowly stirring his coffee, as if he had all the time in the world. She tapped her foot impatiently to remind him she was there.

He turned and came to sit at the table.

'Sometimes you think you know someone, Scarlett. You think you know what they might do in any situation, but people can surprise you – and sometimes disappoint you – even people close to you. It's not always their fault, though. Circumstances can arise...'

Scarlett kept glancing up at the kitchen clock. At the best of times she hated it when adults talked like this: when all the words went together and made sentences but didn't actually say anything.

She wanted to say, *Cut to the chase, Gerry. I've got things to do, places to be,* but she didn't. For once Scarlett held her tongue.

She tuned back in to what Gerry was saying when she suddenly realised all this rambling was about *her dad.*

'...Just because Steve's made some mistakes, doesn't make him a bad person. He must have had his reasons. I'm prepared to trust that; I think you should too. So, that's what I was doing here today, trying to cover his tracks, until we hear from him. So, now you know.'

Scarlett felt like she'd run at forty miles per hour into a brick wall. It winded her and gave her a sick feeling in her stomach. This was far worse than Gerry being after her mum.

'Are you saying it *was* Dad who took this money?'

she gasped, reaching for a chair. Gerry didn't answer, but he didn't deny it either.

Scarlett tried to absorb it all.

'Anyway, I think you should keep this to yourself for now,' he said.

Scarlett still didn't respond, so Gerry went on making excuses for her dad. 'He's probably got into some kind of trouble and can't cope, like that other time. He's just disappeared for a while.'

'Dad hasn't *disappeared*,' Scarlett insisted. 'He's on a boat in the Atlantic!'

'Maybe,' Gerry said, smiling at her, as if she were a much younger child. 'Don't look so scared, Scarlett. You and I both know your dad would never do anything wrong – unless he was backed into a corner. He's not a *villain*…'

The word felt like a physical blow to Scarlett. She stared at Gerry, fiddling with a placemat on the table in front of him. Even now, with her mind racing, Scarlett thought of Mr Coe's simple tasks. She watched Gerry rolling the mat up, then unrolling it, smoothing it flat before rolling it again, each time trying to get it a little tighter. He was giving it all his concentration, rather than look at Scarlett.

She was getting a bad feeling about him, but she still couldn't be sure what she should believe. Scarlett had been wrong so many times lately about other people, about what they were thinking and feeling, sure that she knew exactly what was going on in their heads and then finding she didn't at all. Was it possible she could be as wrong about her *dad*? But her brain immediately rejected the idea. He would *never* take other people's money and she couldn't, she simply *wouldn't*, believe this about him – end of conversation.

But Gerry was still keeping up a conversation with her. 'I don't want you to worry, because I'm going to sort it all out, Scarlett. Whatever your dad's done...'

'*No!*' Scarlett suddenly burst out, surprising herself. She jumped to her feet. 'My dad wouldn't do that. He's not like that. He's...*good.*' It felt such a pathetically inadequate word to use, like *nice* – it didn't begin to describe how she felt about her dad.

Gerry looked up at her, smiling sympathetically. 'I know this is hard for you to get your head round.'

But Scarlett wasn't even prepared to get her head round it. 'Stop it! I don't believe you!' she shouted at Gerry. 'I'm not listening,' she said, clapping her hands over her ears. 'You're lying!'

Gerry's face changed in a second – in a fraction of a second. This face was one Scarlett had never seen before. It was mean. She suddenly recalled Mr Coe's words that morning...*and the mask slips.*

'I don't trust you,' she said, and as if the words had magical power, she felt the whole room changing around her. Even though it was still her own kitchen, it suddenly felt unfamiliar. Everything inside her head was shifting and settling into one clear realisation and it never occurred to Scarlett for a moment that she should keep the thought to herself.

'It was you, wasn't it?' she said. 'You stole that money. I *know*.'

Gerry stared back at her. 'What do you know about anything?' he sneered.

'I know Dad wouldn't have done it,' Scarlett said, stubbornly.

'Oh no, not the Sainted Steve,' Gerry sneered again. 'The perfect husband, brilliant boss, best dad in the world. He'd never do *anything* wrong.'

'I thought you were supposed to be his friend, his best friend. You said...'

'You really shouldn't believe everything people tell you, Scarlett,' Gerry said.

His expression was cold and unpleasant. The tired red rings around his eyes, the sweat on his forehead, the bits he'd missed when he'd shaved, the hard line of his mouth, all made him seem uglier. She hardly recognised him.

Now she could see what Mr Coe had meant when he'd said: *You don't believe that people wear different faces? That they can seem good but be bad?*

Well, she was in no doubt of that any more.

'And you can stop looking at me like that,' Gerry said, as if he were reading her mind. 'You want the truth? The truth is your father's a fool. Don't expect me to feel sorry for him, because I don't. He brought this mess on himself, forever swanning off to Spain with his big ideas and his big plans. Big mistake, wouldn't you say?'

'But he trusted you!' Scarlett snapped. She could feel the tears come from nowhere.

'Yeah,' Gerry laughed. 'That was his biggest mistake.'

Scarlett wanted to jump up and down screaming at the unfairness of it all. She wanted to beat her fists in Gerry's face, but she was too scared of him now to do that. Her good sense was telling her to be very careful about what she said from now on, but she still wanted to understand.

'How could you blame it all on Dad? How could you?' she demanded.

Gerry was so slow to answer she thought he was going to ignore the question, but finally he said, wearily, 'I didn't plan that part. I didn't plan to involve him at all, but when the police came snooping around I had no choice. Believe me, your dad deciding to go off playing Atlantic yachtsman was the first real piece of luck I'd had. But don't worry, Scarlett, he'll land on his feet, the way he always does!'

Scarlett looked at this person she had thought she knew so well – who she'd even thought was her friend. She couldn't believe how he'd kept coming round, being nice to them all – bringing flowers, and DVDs, pretending to be good old Uncle Gerry. Of all the mistakes she'd made about other people, this was the biggest. 'I thought you were my friend,' she said, and immediately heard how pathetic she sounded.

'Oh, grow up, Scarlett,' he snapped. 'I *was* your friend, but things change. Don't take it personally. I've told you, I didn't plan most of this. But once things got out of hand I had to keep coming to find out how much the police knew.'

Scarlett was suddenly desperate to get away from him. She got up to go. 'I've got to get back to school, nobody knows I've gone,' she blurted out, immediately realising she probably shouldn't have told him that.

'*Sit down*, Scarlett,' Gerry told her, in a voice she didn't dare ignore.

Scarlett reluctantly sat down. Gerry barely looked at her, apparently taken up with his own thoughts.

But Scarlett studied him, his shoulders slumped and his forehead creased up with worry. Even though she was the one who felt she couldn't just get up and walk away, Gerry looked trapped too.

Scarlett knew she ought to do something, but she didn't feel brave enough to make a run for it. She couldn't quite believe he would hurt her, even now, but how could she be sure what this *other* Gerry would do? She wished with all her heart he would turn back into the old one: the *good* old Uncle Gerry, and start fooling around with her like he always had done.

After a minute or two, she asked quietly, 'What are you going to do?'

'I don't know!' he yelled at her. 'For God's sake, just stop all the questions. I don't know, all right? I think the police have been watching me. That's why I parked streets away. That's why they came to the house. That's why they'll probably be back. Happy now?'

Scarlett was far from happy, but Gerry's words had given her a scrap of hope. Maybe the police *would* come back. Maybe they were already on their way. While she waited she kept on watching him, trying to guess what he would finally decide to do.

When Gerry next spoke Scarlett could only just hear what he was saying. 'Don't think it's been easy living in your dad's shadow all these years, watching him doing everything right, having the perfect life, while yours runs further and further out of your control. Do you have *any* idea what that feels like?'

Scarlett didn't answer, she just silently shook her head.

'No, I don't suppose you do, Scarlett, any more than your precious dad does. You're so like him, always thinking about yourself.'

Scarlett didn't know what to say to that. She didn't believe it was true of her dad, even if it were true of her.

She went on sitting there in silence, waiting – not a thing Scarlett was very good at. It wasn't long before her tongue got the better of her good sense again.

'What are you going to do with me?' she asked.

This time Gerry didn't shout at her; he said wearily, 'I don't know, Scarlett. I'm running out of ideas.'

Scarlett was short of ideas too, but she couldn't go on just sitting there. 'Can I go to the bathroom?' she asked.

'No,' Gerry said quietly, but firmly.

'I *have* to get back to school,' she almost pleaded with him. 'I borrowed Gemma's bike.'

Gerry's dismissive look left her in no doubt he'd got far more important things on his mind than bikes! Scarlett kicked herself for not being more inventive. She felt sure that heroines in books and plays would have come up with some scheme to distract Gerry, some ingenious plan to rescue themselves. But the truth was that Scarlett was far too scared to do anything heroic or brave – anything that might make Gerry angry again.

She looked up once more at the kitchen clock and her heart sank. It was gone two o'clock. She wondered what was happening at school. Had she been missed at registration? Would Gemma have told anyone where she'd gone?

The silence was nearly killing Scarlett. She noticed how cold she'd gone and that her legs were doing a funny shaking thing. Her skin felt tight and her mouth was dry. This was what it felt like to be really scared, she realised. Her stomach was hurting and she was beginning to feel sick. Tears weren't far away and Scarlett fought to keep them back.

She was still watching Gerry, trying to work out what was going on in his head, when behind him she saw a flicker of movement. Someone was in the garden. *Oh, please, let it be the police,* she prayed.

The next moment she saw DI Maddox signalling to her. He was trying to tell her something. Scarlett screwed up her eyes, desperate to understand what he was indicating. At that very moment Gerry looked up and into her face, and saw that it was creased up in concentration.

'What's the matter?' he asked.

Scarlett had to think fast – she needed a plan. She got out of her chair, clutching her throat dramatically.

'I don't feel well...' she said in a whisper. 'I feel...' Then she collapsed in a faint on the kitchen floor.

Gerry was unimpressed. He'd seen this act far too many times before. 'Get up, Scarlett, and stop fooling about,' he said, standing over her.

But Scarlett didn't get up. She lay there, holding her breath, not moving a muscle. Even then, still feeling terrified, her eyes tightly closed, she couldn't help thinking to herself: this has to be my best performance – *ever!*

Chapter Eighteen

O villain, villain, smiling, damned villain!

Even though he suspected that Scarlett was acting, as usual, Gerry began to panic. He tried to lift her, but Scarlett made herself as heavy as she could, like a dead weight.

'Come on, Scarlett,' he pleaded. 'Don't do this. I didn't mean to scare you; I would never hurt you, you know that. *Please* get up.' He hurried across to the sink, to get her a glass of water.

Scarlett heard the tap running, then she felt him kneeling beside her again, trying to lift her head. Scarlett kept her eyes resolutely closed. She tried to slow her breathing right down, counting slowly to a hundred, wondering how much longer she could keep it up.

Afterwards Scarlett regretted that she hadn't revived herself a moment or two earlier, in time to see the police burst in, to witness the look on Gerry's face. It was only when she heard DI Maddox warning him not to resist arrest that she knew it was safe to open her eyes. She found herself surrounded by four uniformed police officers. The female one bent down to help Scarlett to her feet.

Even with the police there, Scarlett was afraid to actually meet Gerry's eye after so successfully tricking him, but he didn't actually look angry with her. If anything, she thought, he looked as if he was glad it was all over.

'I'd never have hurt her,' he told DI Maddox. 'Tell him, Scarlett, we've always been good friends, haven't we?' He gave her that familiar smile; the mask back in place; the old Gerry returned.

But Scarlett wasn't going to smile back at *him*. In fact, she gave him the kind of icy stare of which Cleo would have been proud.

'I hope I never see you again, you...' But Scarlett couldn't think of a bad enough name to call Gerry. It was only after he'd gone she remembered what Othello calls Iago – *pernicious caitiff*.

Scarlett was surprised, though, that now it was all over, she suddenly felt sorry for him.

The policewoman got her a hot drink, while DI Maddox put a reassuring hand on her shoulder. He was at pains to check she hadn't been hurt in any way.

'You're absolutely sure, now? He didn't do anything to hurt you?'

'No,' Scarlett told him. 'He's not like that.' She'd been scared, more scared than she'd ever been in her life, but she hadn't ever quite believed Gerry would physically hurt her.

'Good,' he said. 'Well, that's a relief anyway. If he had I'd never have forgiven myself.'

'Dad didn't have anything to do with it, you know,' Scarlett told the policeman, wanting to completely clear her father's name. 'It was all Gerry.'

'Oh, we realised that,' he agreed. 'But it was easier to let him think we suspected your dad. By the way, we've finally talked to him.'

'Dad's OK, then?' Scarlett asked excitedly.

'Yes, we spoke to him from the Bahamas. Your mum's had a word too.'

'She didn't tell us!'

'It was only this morning. And, if we'd had any idea you'd be bunking off school, young lady, putting yourself in danger, we might have warned you too. We've been watching Gerry for a couple of days.'

'What's going to happen to him?' Scarlett wanted to know.

'That depends on how far he co-operates.'

'Why do you think he did it?'

'I could only guess at that. Maybe he'll tell us, but there again he may not.'

'That's like Iago,' Scarlett declared. 'He refuses to explain himself right to the end. Miss Kitty says it's his way of hanging onto his power.'

DI Maddox looked impressed, but he was also a little concerned about how excitable Scarlett was getting. 'Do you think you might like to have a little lie down until your mum comes? I've radioed for someone to bring her, she should be here soon.'

Lie down? Scarlett couldn't have lain down just then if her life had depended on it. She was suddenly aware of things she had to do and people she had to see.

'I've got to get Gemma's bike back before the end of school,' she announced.

'No, you don't,' DI Maddox told her, promising to get a message to Gemma. 'You're not going anywhere till your mum's checked you're OK.'

'But what about Drama Club?' Scarlett said, almost frantic. 'Mr Coe's relying on me. It's the first dress rehearsal this afternoon. The whole play depends on me, you know.'

By now even Scarlett could hear herself getting hysterical. Her legs were still shaking, but she didn't feel cold any more – she actually felt as if her face was on fire.

'Maybe your mum will let you go, once she's sure you're OK. We don't want to deprive Mr Coe of your evident talent. But I'll tell you one thing: that fainting fit wouldn't have fooled *me* a second time.'

'No,' said Scarlett, 'but you are a detective inspector.'

'You were very brave, though,' he told her. 'You kept a cool head.'

'I was really scared,' Scarlett admitted, 'but it was quite...' – she wanted to say *exciting*, but it had been a bit too scary for that – '*fascinating*,' she said. 'It's taught me a lot about villains, which will come in very useful for my future career.'

'Don't you fancy playing a goodie, for a change? What about a great detective?'

241

'No-o-o!' said Scarlett, dismissively. 'Villains have all the best lines, you know.'

'Ah, yes,' DI Maddox conceded, 'but they usually come to a sticky end.'

Scarlett's mum took a lot of persuading that Scarlett was fit to go off to her final rehearsal. This was because Scarlett foolishly kept on trying to persuade her mum that she was *absolutely fine, full of beans, never felt better...* But Mum was studying the two bright red spots on Scarlett's cheeks that gave her the look of someone bordering on a fever. Fortunately for Scarlett, she realised just in time to stop ranting and raving and finally calm herself down.

At last her mum agreed to let her go, driving her there in the car and having a few words in private with Mr Coe first. As a result he kept a very close eye on Scarlett throughout the rehearsal.

While the girls were waiting for their cues, Scarlett sat with Gemma, and told her, 'I'm really sorry about your bike.'

Gemma could hardly contain herself. 'What happened? Mr Coe said there'd been a message from the police! Where have you been all afternoon?'

Scarlett hardly knew where to begin. She realised she still wasn't supposed to tell anyone about it, but Gemma *was* her best friend. Surely, Scarlett thought, she couldn't be expected to keep such a great story completely to herself.

'Well,' she sighed, 'you've *absolutely* got to keep this a secret...'

Gemma nodded solemnly.

'It was just like something on TV,' Scarlett began. 'There I was, all on my own in an empty house, with Uncle Gerry, who's suddenly turned into this horrible, creepy, criminal...and he's holding me *hostage*...'

Gemma gasped, which Scarlett found most gratifying.

'He's stolen all this money from dad's clients,' she continued. 'I mean *mega*-amounts...'

'How much?' Gemma wanted to know.

'Dunno, probably millions...gazillions even...'

Gemma gasped again.

'So he's got me *hostage*...' Scarlett couldn't resist repeating the word.

'Did he have a gun?' Gemma asked, slightly spoiling Scarlett's flow.

'Nooo,' she said, ''Course not. But he won't let me move. Not even to go to the bathroom. He's just sitting there, staring at me, trying to decide what he's going to do with me... Maybe go on the run and take me with him...'

Gemma gasped again. 'What happened next?'

It was deeply frustrating for both of them that Scarlett had to break off at such a gripping moment, but Mr Coe was calling for them.

'It's a very long story,' Scarlett told Gemma, as they took their places, 'but I'll tell you *all* the gory details later.'

'I could come round tonight after we finish,' Gemma tentatively suggested. 'You said you'd help me with my lines.'

'OK,' Scarlett agreed. 'Perhaps you can help me with mine.'

Gemma looked sceptical for a moment. 'Since when did you ever need any help?'

'Everyone needs help sometimes,' Scarlett admitted.

At the end of the dress rehearsal Mr Coe told Scarlett he was *utterly amazed* at the transformation, but he wished she hadn't left it until the eleventh hour. 'You've probably taken weeks off my life, Scarlett Lee,' he lightly scolded her. 'But I should have known you'd rise to the challenge in the end.'

Later that evening, after Gemma had left, Scarlett and Cleo and their mum were once again in the kitchen, this time making double chocolate chip cookies – Scarlett's favourite. After the day's excitement everyone felt in need of a little baking therapy. They had just finished their long-awaited phone call with Dad, who would soon be on a flight home. Until he was safely back they had agreed not to worry him with Scarlett's *little adventure*, as Mum was now calling it.

When the cookies were ready for the oven, Mum put two trays in to bake, while Cleo started the clearing up.

'I still can't believe it all,' Scarlett told her mum, licking the spoon.

'I can,' Cleo said. 'I'd had a bad feeling about *him* since the moment we heard about dad's trip.'

'Poor old Gerry,' Mum said, shaking her head.

'How can you say that?' Cleo demanded.

'Well, he must have been desperate. You have

to admit he's had it hard, with Patti an invalid and his girls always away at school.'

'And that excuses him?' Cleo snapped. 'The minute Dad turns his back Gerry stabs him in it.'

'I don't think he planned that bit,' Scarlett said, running her finger round the bowl.

'Don't *you* try to defend him,' Cleo warned, taking the bowl from her.

'Well, I think Scarlett's right,' Mum agreed. 'He got in over his head. He started buying shares in a company that was about to be taken over, with money he'd borrowed from clients' accounts.'

'*Borrowed*?' said Cleo, sceptically. 'Nice one.'

'But when the takeover fell through the shares dropped in price and he had to make the money up somehow. So he borrowed again and again...'

'Why didn't he just *stop*?' Cleo asked.

'It's like gambling, I guess,' said Mum. 'He kept thinking that next time he'd have more luck.'

'He got in a hole and the more he dug the deeper he got,' said Scarlett, wisely. 'Like Mr Coe says: one bad action led to another.'

Mum and Cleo both looked at Scarlett, raising their eyebrows.

'Mr Coe wasn't talking about Gerry,' Scarlett quickly explained. 'He meant Iago. But I think it was the same thing.'

Mum smiled. 'Yes, I think so, too. Once the police began a fraud investigation he panicked and tried to shift the blame onto Dad. He even opened an off-shore bank account in Dad's name.'

'How long have you known all this?' Cleo asked, suspiciously.

'And why didn't you tell us?' Scarlett demanded.

Their mum began to hedge. 'DI Maddox asked me not to say anything...in case Gerry realised they were on to him.'

'And you thought *we* couldn't keep the secret?' Cleo asked, offended.

'*I'm* supposed to be the actress in this family!' Scarlett reminded her mum.

'Clearly not the only one,' Mum said proudly.

After the rehearsal, Mr Coe said that if we do that well tomorrow it will have been our BEST PERFORMANCE EVER. He says we all grew six inches. Brogan said: chance would be a fine thing. But I said to her: he didn't mean it LITERALLY, you doughnut.

I have decided that where acting's concerned
I agree with Mr Coe AND Miss Kitty.
Miss Kitty was right when she said I didn't
need to be a villain to play one. But it
was seeing Gerry and what a horrible
person he turned into through his ENVY AND
RESENTMENT that really helped me understand
Iago. So I agree with Mr Coe: you need to
bring your own life into your acting too. My
life has certainly been a lot more exciting
lately, which is bound to make me a better
actress from now on...

I wonder what our next play will be? Mr Coe
wouldn't tell us, but he said mine and
Gemma's audition had given him an idea! Oh,
I would DIE to play Lady Macbeth. Out,
damned spot! Out, I say!

Now THAT could be MY BEST PERFORMANCE EVER!

On Friday evening Scarlett and Gemma peeped out
from behind the curtain, trying to spot people they

knew in the audience. In one row were Gemma's parents, her grandma and grandad, her sister and her sister's boyfriend. Sitting behind them, Scarlett spotted her mum and Cleo, and Miss Kitty, wearing a very strange turban. Beside her was DI Maddox and, to Scarlett's amazement, PC Dryer! He was leaning forward, pretending to tie his shoelaces, but she could tell he was really trying to get a glimpse of Cleo further down the row.

Scarlett's dad wasn't there but he'd promised he'd be at the Saturday night performance – jetlag or not. Scarlett could see her mum looking a little nervous. She was probably worrying whether Scarlett would remember all her lines.

Cleo was frowning, too, and Scarlett couldn't decide if this was Cleo's *please-don't-let-Scarlett-do-anything-outrageous-and-embarrass-us* face, or more likely, her *what-is-that-idiot-boy-doing-staring-at-me-and-I-wish-he-would-stop* face.

When Scarlett relayed all this to Gemma, she couldn't stop giggling. Finally the two girls were the best of friends again – if not quite back on their old terms, at least on new ones. Scarlett had learned a lot of useful things listening to Gerry, some that were going to help her acting, but others that had made her think about her friendships too.

Scarlett couldn't help it if she was a confident and enthusiastic actress, if she was sometimes a bit OTT, or as Cleo said, *in your face*. That was just who she was and she wasn't going to change that much. But Scarlett could see that sometimes she could be more sensitive around her friends, especially Gemma.

Already she had been trying to make up for it, giving Gemma lots of encouragement, telling her how well she was playing Roderigo. And it was already making a difference, especially to Gemma's nerves. Lots of the other girls were in a far worse state.

For the last hour Scarlett had been doing her best to calm them all down.

'Chill, chill,' she advised them. 'Go with the flow...'

'It's all right for you. *You've* probably never had nerves in your life,' Abbie told Scarlett, almost physically sick with hers.

'She probably wouldn't know them if they came and bit her on the bum,' Leah agreed.

But for the first time Scarlett *was* aware of nerves. She'd been brushing her hair until it crackled with electricity. When Mr Coe insisted it was all tied up and hidden under a cap she hadn't known what to do with her hands. It was a new experience for Scarlett and it reminded her of the times she'd been on rollercoaster rides and felt as if she had a big empty hole in her stomach.

Scarlett, however, had the advantage of Miss Kitty's helpful advice on the subject and was trying to share it now with the other girls.

'You have to take deep breaths, that's the secret,' she told them. 'In for ten, hold for three, out for ten. Watch me.'

Scarlett demonstrated the technique as all her friends stood facing her, breathing in and breathing out – some, like Brogan, faster than others and sounding like a steam train, but all of them *gradually* calming down.

Mr Coe watched and smiled to himself. Then, with only moments before the curtain opened, he gathered them all together to give them a final pep talk. It was one the girls had heard before but it never failed to inspire Scarlett.

'You've all worked very hard. Now I want you to go out there and enjoy yourselves. Work as a team, stay focused and give it *plenty of fizz*! But try to notice the moment when it all comes together, when you slip into the world of the play, forgetting everything else around you, losing yourselves completely, because that, girls, is *THE JOY OF ACTING*.'

Scarlett and Gemma took their places on stage and waited for the curtains to open. In the darkness and silence, in that moment before the lights came up, Scarlett reached out and squeezed Gemma's hand.

Under her breath she whispered, over and over again, 'Oh, joy! Oh, joy! Oh, joy...'

Quotations used in this book

Chapter One
'All the world's a stage,
And all the men and women merely players...'
– *As You Like It*, William Shakespeare

Chapter Two
'Though this be madness, yet there is method in't.'
– *Hamlet*, William Shakespeare

Chapter Three
'O, beware, my lord, of jealousy;
It is the green-eyed monster which doth mock
The meat it feeds on...'
– *Othello*, William Shakespeare

Chapter Four
'A horse! A horse! My kingdom for a horse!'
– *Richard III*, with apologies to William Shakespeare

Chapter Five
'There are no small parts, only small actors.'
— Konstantin Stanislavski

Chapter Six
'This was the most unkindest cut of all...'
– *Julius Caesar*, William Shakespeare

Chapter Seven
'Now is the winter of our discontent
Made glorious summer by this son of York...'
– *Richard III*, William Shakespeare

Chapter Eight
'Art mirrors life.'
— Unattributed

Chapter Nine
'I am a man
More sinn'd against than sinning.'
– *King Lear*, William Shakespeare

Chapter Ten
'You should try acting, my boy. It's much easier.'
— Laurence Olivier to Dustin Hoffman

Chapter Eleven
'When sorrows come, they come not single spies,
But in battalions.'
– *Hamlet*, William Shakespeare

Chapter Twelve
'Oh God, that men should put an enemy in their mouths to steal away
their brains!'
– *Othello*, William Shakespeare

Chapter Thirteen
'Exit, pursued by a bear.'
– Stage direction in *The Winter's Tale*, William Shakespeare

Chapter Fourteen
'Life is better with a little drama in it!'
– Scott Nilsson, actor

Chapter Fifteen
'Ay, now the plot thickens very much upon us.'
– *The Rehearsal*, George Villiers, 2nd Duke of Buckingham (politician and
writer)

Chapter Sixteen
By the pricking of my thumbs,
Something wicked this way comes.
– *Macbeth*, William Shakespeare

Chapter Seventeen
'I'll pour this pestilence into his ear,
...So will I turn her virtue into pitch,
And out of her own goodness make the net
That shall enmesh them all.'
– *Othello*, William Shakespeare

Chapter Eighteen
'O villain, villain, smiling, damned villain!'
– *Hamlet*, William Shakespeare

More Orchard Red Apples

Pink Chameleon	Fiona Dunbar	978 1 84616 230 5*
River Song	Belinda Hollyer	978 1 84362 943 6*
The Truth About Josie Green	Belinda Hollyer	978 1 84362 885 9
The Shooting Star	Rose Impey	978 1 84362 560 5
Hothouse Flower	Rose Impey	978 1 84616 215 2
My Scary Fairy Godmother	Rose Impey	978 1 84362 683 1
Forever Family	Gill Lobel	978 1 84616 211 4*
Do Not Read This Book	Pat Moon	978 1 84121 435 1
Do Not Read Any Further	Pat Moon	978 1 84121 456 6
Do Not Read Or Else	Pat Moon	978 1 84616 082 0

Priced at £4.99. Those marked * are £5.99.

Orchard Red Apples are available from all good bookshops, or can be ordered direct
from the publisher: Orchard Books, PO BOX 29, Douglas IM99 1BQ
Credit card orders please telephone 01624 836000
or fax 01624 837033 or visit our Internet site: www.wattspub.co.uk
or e-mail: bookshop@enterprise.net for details.

To order please quote title, author and ISBN
and your full name and address.
Cheques and postal orders should be made payable to 'Bookpost plc.'
Postage and packing is FREE within the UK
(overseas customers should add £1.00 per book).

Prices and availability are subject to change.